laura miller

national best-selling author of *The Life We Almost Had*

when
cicadas cry

a love story

Love isn't
SUPPOSED TO BE PAINLESS.
IT'S SUPPOSED TO BE *worth it*

This book is a work of fiction. Names, characters, businesses, places and incidents are the product of the author's imagination or are used fictitiously. Any resemblance to actual events, locals or persons, living or dead, is coincidental.

Copyright © 2015 by Laura Miller.

When Cicadas Cry
LauraMillerBooks.com

ISBN-13: 978-1507570173
ISBN-10: 1507570171

Printed in the United States of America.

Cover design by Laura Miller.
Cover photos © luizclas.
Title page photos © luizclas.
Dedication page photo © Africa Studio/Fotolia.
Content page photo © Africa Studio/Fotolia.
Quote pages photo © Africa Studio/Fotolia.
Second title page photo © Africa Studio/Fotolia.
Chapter headings photo © Africa Studio/Fotolia.
Torn page photo © ba1969/rgbstock.
Torn page design by Laura Miller.
Acknowledgments page photo © Africa Studio/Fotolia.
Author photo © Neville Miller.

To the Author of mortals,
For the greater dance

CONTENTS

Time flies over us but leaves its shadow behind.

~Nathaniel Hawthorne

To Jean,

When Cicadas Cry

a novel

LAURA MILLER

It's worth it!

Laura Miller

When I saw you, I fell in love, and you smiled because you knew.

~William Shakespeare

Prologue

Ashley

One moment.

One moment can shape our entire life.

One deep breath.

One slow exhale.

The first time you feel soft grass on your bare feet.

The last time you fell in love.

One painted sunrise.

A note in a song.

One line in a poem.

Your first shot of whiskey.

One taste of forbidden love.

One word spoken too soon.

One word spoken too late.

Your first heartbreak.
One dance with a stranger.
One smile.
One look.
One thought.
One wayward memory.
One secret kept just a moment too long.
That's all it takes.

My grandmother had a lot of little phrases she liked to say to my sister and me when we were growing up. Like when she'd catch us staring out the window too long—those times when she'd have to say our names at least twice before we'd answer—she'd always say: *If you want to know where your heart is, look to where your mind goes when it wanders.*

I never had to look too far.

My heart is with him; it has been, since Day One.

But what I didn't know when we locked eyes that first time was that every moment we shared was just another moment leading up to that one that would forever change the course of our lives.

It was the moment that I knew he *knew.*

It was just a hunch, a feeling, a soft whisper to my soul. But it was in that moment—that one, life-altering instant—that I knew I had lost him.

And so began our story.

Chapter One

Present

Rem

"Sorry, man," I hear a voice say.

A guy turns into me and then backs off. I don't say anything; I just keep pushin' my way through the swaying masses of blue jeans and tee shirts and work boots. Hall's is crowded tonight. The stools at the old, wooden bar top are full. The few tables scattered around the bar are also occupied, and the little space left is taken up by stragglers, craning their necks to get a glimpse of one of only two small TVs in the whole place. The game's on—third game of the World Series. And that's why I'd like to get my order and get the hell out of here. At least back home, there's a TV screen that isn't straight out of the 90s.

"Wait."

I turn back toward the voice. It's the man I just ran into...or who just ran into me; I don't know. He's staring at me, but I don't recognize the guy. He's got this funny grin on his face, and he's wagging a finger at me.

"You...and Ashley Westcott..." He nods his head as if he's just put two and two together.

"No," I say. "Wrong guy."

I turn back toward the bar even though I'm pretty sure he's still starin' and pointin'. Karen notices me and holds out a brown paper bag.

"Here ya go, Rem." She gives me a motherly kind of smile. I know she heard the guy, and she probably heard what I had to say to him too, but I don't care.

"Keep the change," I say, handing her a bill.

I reach for the bag, but she keeps a firm grip on it and settles her gaze on me.

"It gets better." She smiles and lets go of the bag.

I don't say anything, and I try not to react either. I just tip the bill of my cap and head straight for the screen door in the corner of the bar.

Seconds later, my hand is pushin' against the old, wooden frame. The door squeaks open and then slams shut behind me.

Outside, the October air is cool. I feel it sink deep into my bones, and at the same time, a shiver runs up my spine. And I'm not really sure if it's the cold or the thoughts runnin' through my head that cause it. Either way, it feels a whole hell of a lot better out here than it did in that crowded bar; that's for sure. At least, out here, there ain't anyone makin' any assumptions. Out here, no one's givin' me sympathetic smiles or coverin' up their whispers. The black night doesn't care she's gone.

I stop and rest my hand on the door handle of my truck, and I let my head fall back. The sky is darker than dark, but the stars are bright.

We had this whole town fooled. Every. Last. One. Even now, they just don't know what to think. Half of them constantly have a question on their tongues, but it's as if they just can't quite get it to leave their mouths. And I'm convinced the other half already has their minds made up—even though I'm pretty sure not a darned one knows the story.

I level my head and catch a star dyin' out in the distant sky. In an instant, it's there, and then it's gone. I lower my head and laugh a little. *Just like us, huh?*

Then I sigh and pull on the handle right before I toss the bag onto the seat and slide into my truck. But as soon as I get the key in the ignition, I stop, and I think about the guy in the bar. And I think about her. *Her.*

"Damn it, Miss Westcott," I whisper under my breath. "I swear I can't go anywhere without you. Everywhere I go, you're always just a rumor away."

I let a lungful of air fall onto the steering wheel as I put the truck in gear and let off the clutch.

You left, but then again, you never really left.

Chapter Two

Past (2 Years Earlier)

Ashley

"*T*he whole town already thinks we're in love." He bends down low and almost whispers the phrase into my ear. I don't know what else to do but smile, so I do that.

He finds my eyes once more. I've been locking gazes with him from across this space all night, and now, my heart races. I don't know if I expected him to come over here. I wanted him to, I think, but I also didn't think he would.

Without saying another word, he holds out his hand and eyes the little dance floor. It's just a little hardwood floor, surrounded by a sea of soft, cool grass and lit only by the stars and a couple strands of little white lights.

I look around and notice the eyes planted on the two of us. I don't know how long they've been staring, but I can't help but notice the ease at which their eyes roam over us.

It's almost as if their stares come as naturally as breathing. I feel almost like an exhibit at an art gallery, where everyone is trying to read into the meaning of every detail. But then I look back into his eyes, and the burden of being watched suddenly disappears. In this moment, this perfect stranger is all that matters.

"Well, let's not disappoint them then," I say, surrendering my hand.

He smiles at me, and I can't help but smile back. And as he stands there—his eyes never leaving mine—I study him. I study the way his lips slowly, but gradually turn up—in a way that lets me know he might be used to smiles from the opposite persuasion. I study the way his eyes stare back at me, as if we both share some kind of secret, and we both know it, but neither one of us is going to be the first to tell. And yet, there's still something else about him that I just can't put my finger on. And it's that something else that makes me feel as if I can trust him. I don't know if it's on his lips or in his eyes or written somewhere on his face, but somehow, he's got this way about him that makes me feel as if it's all going to be okay. And it's this way about him, I think, that makes me wish I knew him more...or at all.

He gently takes my hand and leads me out to the middle of the dance floor. I can feel the eyes follow us there. I can feel them as if they're literally a weight on my shoulder. I sense them speculating, assuming. They don't even know us, and it's as if they're already pulling for us...or against us. But little do they know, we're not even an us.

"Ashley Westcott."

My eyes immediately dart to his shadowed face as he turns to me, rests one palm on my lower back and gently draws me closer to him. "How did you...?"

"Just trust me on this one." He smiles and then looks away. "It's one of those things that by growin' up here, you just know."

"But I'm not..."

"I know," he says, nodding his head. "That's how I know your name...because you're not from here." His eyes meet mine, and this time, I take notice of their color. They're this light kind of bluish green—the kind that makes you a little seasick just looking at them.

"So you know everyone's name around here?" I ask.

He seems to pause as he drops his gaze to the floor. "Pretty much, but yours in particular."

I laugh once. I don't know if I'm nervous or flattered that this stranger knows my name. He finds my eyes again. And despite the fact that I'm still trying to figure him out, my lips involuntarily turn up. "Does my reputation precede me?"

He sucks in a big breath and then slowly nods. "I'm afraid it does."

My heart instantly plummets in my chest. And I think it must show on my face because there's a subtle shift in his expression. Does he know? I take a quick survey of the room. Their eyes are still on us, but now, I'm wondering if their eyes are really just on me.

"In a good way," he clarifies. "In a good way," he repeats."

I search his new expression. He's showing off his white teeth in a big smile, and from what I can tell, there's not an ounce of hesitation in his eyes. I silently say a thankful prayer. He doesn't know.

Several heartbeats pass between us, as I gently bite my bottom lip in an attempt to keep it all together. But all the while, I still manage to keep a watchful eye on him. Him. *I still don't know his name.*

"Remington," he says, as if reading my mind. "My name is Remington, but you can call me Rem."

I start to ask the obvious question—how he knew I was thinking about his name—but it never leaves my tongue. Instead, I just smile at him. "Do you have a last name, Remington?" I glance down at our feet before finding his eyes again. "You know mine. I think it's only fair that I should know yours."

"Of course." His grin slowly reaches his eyes. "It's Jude. Remington Jude."

"Well, it's nice to meet you, Remington Jude."

He bobs his head once. "Likewise, Miss Westcott."

I try not to blush. I hate it when I blush; it gives away everything I'm trying to hide.

Suddenly, I feel him pulling me closer. I don't resist because I want this to feel normal, even though it doesn't, even though it still feels new and strange and wonderful.

"I think we just made them believers, Miss Westcott," he breathes into my ear.

I look up. There's several couples surrounding us now, swaying back and forth to the old slow song, but most are only on the outskirts, and their hands are to their faces, as if they're trying to hide the thoughts pouring out of their mouths.

"Is it always like this?"

"What?" he asks. "The curiosity?"

"Yes." I laugh. "If you can call it that."

"Yeah, pretty much." His eyes trail to the people lining the dance floor before finding me again. "Most get used to it. You probably will too...if you plan on stayin' awhile."

I feel my lips turning up because I have no plans of leaving any time soon. I needed a change of pace. This place is a change of pace all right. And I needed a dance in a town I don't know with a boy I really don't know either. I needed this.

The slow song fades away, but he continues to hold me against his warm body. And he doesn't just hold me. He holds me tightly, securely, as if he's afraid I'll run. His arms are strong—wide and muscular. It almost makes me dizzy thinking about how one of those arms is currently wrapped around my waist and how only a thin layer of fabric separates his skin from mine.

"Maybe next year," he whispers in my ear, "we can give them an even bigger show."

His raspy whisper surprises me and sends chills through my core. I look up and catch an older woman smiling at us from a table in the corner. "Oh," I say, trying to sound unfazed by the hypnotizing way his sultry voice moved through me, "and what did you have in mind?"

"I don't know." He pulls away so that I can see his face and the sea-colored waves in his eyes. "Maybe we could actually come to the dance together, or at least, sit at the same table. That'll get 'em talkin'."

I laugh once. "Getting a little ahead of ourselves, aren't we?" I look away before finding his eyes again. "I mean, coming together is one thing. But sitting at the same table? That might be moving a little too fast for me."

He chuckles a little. I like that I've made him laugh. He's even cuter when he laughs.

"Well, maybe I can just settle for a table on the same side of the room then. Then, I wouldn't have to dodge so many heads tryin' to catch your glance."

I lower my eyes and laugh softly to myself, as he backs away, still holding my hand. "It was an honor makin' rumors with you, Ashley Westcott."

I lift my gaze back into his eyes. "Anytime, Remington Jude."

And even as I say the words, I know I mean them. For the first time in a really long time, I feel as if it might not be so bad to fall head over heels for a beautiful stranger. And maybe it's because he doesn't feel like a stranger at all, really. In fact, nothing about this town feels strange. It's almost as if I was always meant to find myself here. I mean, this place isn't anything like home—even down to the red clay stuck to the bottom of my shoes—and yet, I feel as if I don't belong anywhere but here.

Chapter Three

Past

Rem

"So, I met the girl last night."

"What girl?" Jack looks up from his phone, swivels around in my kitchen chair and faces me. "Ohhhh...the girl?"

I just smile and nod.

"Well, did she live up to your crazy fantasy?" He goes back to fiddlin' with the screen on his phone.

"Even better," I say, grabbin' a can of soda out of the fridge.

"What? You've gotta be kiddin' me?" He tosses the phone onto the table. "Really?"

"Yeah, really. She was at the dance, and she was wearin' this short, little dress, but not too short...you know?"

*He nods as if confirming he knows what I'm talkin'
about.*

*"Anyway, she was beautiful. It was seriously like a
dream."*

*"Well, I'll be," he says, leanin' back and liftin' his
front, two chair legs off the floor.*

*"Yeah, she came with a friend, I think. And she was
sweet and easy to talk to."*

"So you actually talked to her this time?"

"Even better; I danced with her."

*Jack doesn't say anything at first. He just looks at me
with his dumb mouth agape. "No shit?"*

*I shrug my shoulders and just keep smilin'—because I
can't seem to stop.*

*"Well, hot damn!" He gets up and walks over to the
fridge. "All these months of stalkin' her actually paid off."*

"I wasn't stalkin' her."

*He stops and looks up at me with a straight, sober look
on his face. "Buddy, you go to the grocery store on Saturday
afternoon. Saturday afternoon! You know how many games
are on Saturday afternoons?" He opens the refrigerator and
pulls out a can. "But you go there because you know she'll
be there. We all know it. And that, my friend," he says,
holding up a finger, "is stalkin' at its finest." He pulls the
tab and leans up against the fridge.*

*"All right, all right, whatever." I take a drink. "You
know, you did miss one hell of a party last night."*

*"Aw, you know I don't care for that shit. Yeah, the
band's all right, but that's just another way for this town to
keep tabs on ya."*

*I laugh once and shake my head. "You're just like
Owen."*

*He stops mid-sip and lowers his can from his mouth.
"Yeah, well he had it right."*

*With that, I take a deep breath, force out a sigh and just
nod, as silent moments take over the space around us.*

12

"So, what is this mysterious girl's name again?" Jack asks, squashing the quiet.

"Ashley," I say. "Ashley Westcott."

"Yeah, that's right. So where's she from?"

I sit down and think about it. "I don't think she ever said. But I don't think she's from a small town. I think all the eyes kind of weirded her out."

"A big-city girl. No shit?"

"Must be."

"So when are you seein' her next?"

I chuckle and shake my head. "I guess next Saturday at the grocery store."

Jack laughs to himself and then walks over to the table again and sits down across from me.

"But this time, I'm askin' her out."

"Shit, if you don't ask her Saturday, I think I will, just to put you out of your damn misery."

"Aw, no," I say, leanin' back in my chair. "This ain't misery. This is the chase. This, my friend, is the best part."

Jack shakes his head, lookin' as if he's tryin' to swallow down a grin. "Shit. Whatever you say, buddy. Whatever. You. Say."

Chapter Four

Present

I get through the door and immediately hear their usual dumb, loud chants about the food bein' here.

I toss the brown paper bag onto the coffee table, which is really just the box the TV came in, and the chants instantly stop.

"What'd I miss?" I ask, watchin' as their focus now turns to the bag of cheeseburgers.

"Holiday. Base hit," Jack says, tearin' into the packaging around his dinner.

I grab a burger too and fall into my chair. They all know they're welcome at my house anytime, but they all know they can't sit in my chair.

"Damn it," Jack says, hittin' his palm against his

thigh. "A base hit, and they throw it away."

It looks as if it's the third out and the bottom of the inning, from what I can tell. And before I can figure anything else out, the game goes to a commercial break.

"They've gotta win this one," Mike says, from across the room. "We don't want to have to win in Detroit."

Detroit. It's like a dirty word. Just the sound of it makes us all sit in some kind of weird nervous state, gnawin' on our burgers and thinkin' about the possibility of losin' this game.

"Oh, yeah," Jack says, suddenly relievin' our anxiousness, "tomorrow night, Tommy's workin', so I'm havin' him bring pizzas to the house for the game."

The house. I chuckle a little at that. I don't know when the hell my house became *the house*. I don't see any of their names on the mortgage.

"Yeah!" Mike stands up and high fives Jack before he reaches into the bag and pulls out another burger. "I love your little bro, man. AND his job!"

"Yeah, he's good for somethin', at least," Jack says.

"Hey, remember I won't be here," I interject.

They all look at me as if I've just announced that I won't be able to make it to my own funeral or somethin'. They've both got these confused-as-hell looks on their faces. It takes a second, but it finally hits them...or maybe just Jack. Mike looks to be back in his own little world—the one where only a burger and a TV exist.

"Oh, yeah." Jack sits back in the couch again. "You've got that fancy business meeting tomorrow." He waves me off with his hand.

I try to choke down a laugh. Fancy to these guys is a coffee table that isn't a cardboard box. "Uh, yeah, so I'll be back Thursday. Just try not to wreck the place."

"Nah," Mike says, shakin' his head. At the same

time, he winks at Jack. "We'd never do that."

I roll my eyes and laugh once. These two are the type of guys that will steal your wallet and then help you look for it. I don't know why I agreed to play ball with them in the first place that hot summer afternoon in '98. We were just five years old at the time, but damn, you'd think I'd have a little better judgment at that age. Anyway, the first time I came back from a work meeting, I pulled up to the whole town havin' a party, which would have been just fine. The only problem was that they were all hangin' out at 207 Walnut Road—my house. Really, I was pissed for about as long as it took me to get from my truck to the back porch. After a long flight and a long drive home, all I wanted to do was sit back in my old chair, drink a beer and fall asleep. That was until I saw that beautiful blonde sittin' on my porch swing. She saved these guys from an ass-beatin', that's for sure. I really would have done it had she not been there.

Back then, Ashley Westcott was the love of my life. ...But then, that was a long time ago, I guess.

"So, you'll be back Thursday?" Jack asks.

I shake my head as if shaking myself out of some deep daydream or somethin', and then I look up at Jack. "Yeah," I say, without givin' it any thought. "Thursday."

Chapter Five

Past (2 Years Earlier)

"Damn it!" I step on a beer can and have to pry it from my dress shoe. "Where in the hell is Jack?" I say the words out loud, but I'm pretty sure no one's even in earshot to hear them.

I make my way up the steps to the back porch. And all of a sudden, I notice there are people everywhere—linin' the wooden railin', leanin' up against the house, in the backyard.

"Rem." I feel a hand cling to my bicep, and immediately, I smell a combination of alcohol and some strong flowery scent...maybe perfume. "This is such a great party." Stacey says the words so close to my ear that I can feel her hot breaths tickle my skin. "I didn't know you were having a party tonight until just this afternoon."

I don't smile. I can't. "Yeah, well, I didn't either."

She gives me a half-confused look, which quickly turns into a kind-of-seductive smile, and then she squeezes my bicep again. I'm definitely not in the mood for this, so I take another step and feel her hand fall from my arm. Where the hell is Jack?

And then I see her.

I stop mid-stride. I suck in a quick breath. I feel my heart speed up a notch. And just like that, I forget about Jack. I forget about all the people at my house. I even forget I'm mad. I forget everything but her.

I notice her blond hair and her pretty face first. She's sittin' on the porch swing—my porch swing—and she's laughin' and talkin' to two girls I've never seen before. I look down at myself. I'm still in the clothes I had on in my meeting today—black slacks and a white dress shirt, though the shirt's top two buttons are undone, and the shirt's untucked now. And I've got my favorite leather jacket on and an old, faded Cardinals baseball cap fitted over my head.

I brush off my pants like I'm brushin' crumbs away, even though I haven't had anything to eat since Austin. And when I'm through with that, I stealthily slide open the glass door that leads into the house. I'm tryin' to be quiet, so she doesn't notice me. I just got nervous, all of a sudden. And maybe if I stall a little bit, the nerves will go away...or at the very least, maybe I'll catch my breath again.

I set my bag inside on the floor. Then I pause for a moment to lift my cap and run my fingers through my hair. I'm hopin' it buys me a few, extra seconds and gives me a moment to think about what I'm gonna say.

"Remington Jude." A sweet, familiar voice hangs in the lukewarm air, even before I can lift a foot in her direction. She says the words as if she were waiting for me or as if we were old friends or somethin'. I'm just happy she remembers my name.

"Ashley Westcott," I say, tippin' my cap and returning

18

the greeting.

She smiles wide and then sets her drink down onto one of the wooden planks that make up the floor. "Rem, these are my friends, Erin and Katie. Erin and Katie, this is Rem."

"Hi," I say to both of them at once.

They smile back at me, but then, a few moments pass, and no one says a thing. My mind is scramblin' to think of words—any damn words.

"Wait, so how do you two know each other?" the brunette, who I think is Erin, asks.

"Oh," Ashley says, lookin' up at me. "We don't really. We were just feeding the rumor mill last weekend." She smiles at me. It's the sweetest smile I've ever seen. My heart damn near melts.

"Oh," the girl says. A confused and suspicious look stretches across her face. And for several more awkward moments, no one says a thing.

"Well," the brunette interjects, breaking the silence for a second time, "I guess we'll leave you guys to it then." It sounds like a statement, but it also could be a question.

Ashley smiles at Erin, and then I notice Erin squeeze Ashley's hand. And then Erin and Katie take their drinks and make their way to the other corner of the deck where there's a group of guys I know from high school huddled up. They're probably talkin' about some mundane thing about work or some blown call in the last baseball game. Little do they know, their night's about to get a little more interesting.

"Well, you dressed up."

"What?" My attention falls back on her. And I know I've got this dumb look on my face, at least until I connect the dots. "Oh, well, you know, I like to wear my best for parties like this."

I notice her look around a little, and at the same time, press her lips together, as if she's tryin' not to smile.

"Somebody's gotta class up this place," I say. "And Dusty over there in his dirty overalls sure isn't gonna do it."

She looks over at Dusty and then back into my eyes for a brief moment before she laughs.

"Nah," I say then, with a crooked smile. "Actually, I just got here. I came from a work meeting." And without another thought, I fall into one of the empty lawn chairs across from her.

She gives me a disbelieving look and then glances at her watch. "It's awfully late for a meeting."

"Yeah." It's all I can think to say. I'm too busy tryin' to wipe the damn smile off my face, knowin' that my night just got a little more interesting, too.

"Please tell me you're not into something bad."

"What?" And as soon as I say the word, I put it all together. "No," I say, shakin' my head. "No, not bad." I sit back and slowly lift a finger. I feel some confidence rising up from somewhere deep in my chest all of a sudden. "You know, marijuana is legal in four states."

"Yeah," she says, "but not this one."

Her smile instantly twists into a frown, as if she's disappointed, as if she expected more from me. I don't know why, but that kind of makes me feel good. And it takes everything in me to choke down a laugh. "I'm kidding. I was in Austin this mornin'—the meeting. I just got off the plane. Well, I just got off the plane two hours ago."

"Oh," she says. I think she starts to blush. Her cheeks get a little red. I love that there's some warm blood in those blue veins of hers.

"The joys of livin' in a small town," I add. "Airports are a little hard to come by."

Her sweet smile returns, and it's even prettier the second time around. "So I've noticed."

Then we're both quiet, and for the first time since we started talkin', I remember that there are still people all around us, laughin', drinkin', havin' conversations—some louder than others. It's funny; I don't even notice they're here when we're talkin'.

"You know," she says, bringin' me back to her, "I just moved here not too long ago, but this is the first party I've been to here. I thought it was about time to start mingling with the locals."

I smile at her choice of words. For some reason, when I think of the word locals, *it makes me think of a bunch of bushmen livin' off the land in some remote part of the world or somethin'. ...Then again, I guess it's not too far off, really.*

"I met your buddy over there." She points in between two slats in the porch railing to a place in the backyard. I turn around to see who she's pointin' at. It's Jack. And instead of cursing his name, I laugh. It's funny how quickly I forgot I wanted to kick his ass.

"And," she goes on, "he invited me and my friends here tonight."

"Did he now?" I ask, givin' her my full attention again.

She nods. "Yeah, well, he invited everyone in the Conoco gas station up the road. I just happened to be there."

"That little shit!"

"What?" she asks. I can tell she's a little startled by my outburst.

I study her for a moment. She's got this completely innocent look on her face. And I figure out quickly that she has no idea.

"Do you know who lives here?" I ask.

Her small smile starts to fade before she bites at her bottom lip and shrugs her shoulders. I think that just might be my new favorite look of hers—if I had to pick. "No," she says, shaking her head. "I think I just assumed it was his. Is that bad?"

I look down at the wooden floor and chuckle to myself. "No, not at all. In fact," I say, lookin' back up, "I'm sure the guy who lives here is pretty happy you're here."

Her eyes instantly narrow, and her beautiful smile

returns in full effect. "You?"

I was never really good at poker because everything is pretty much always written on my face. "I can't take credit for the party, though," I confess. "What I can take credit for, maybe, is my poor ability to choose good friends."

She laughs, and at the same time, picks up her glass and takes a drink. "Well, it's a nice house," she says.

"Thanks," I say, suddenly feelin' awkward.

But the awkwardness doesn't last long. In the next heartbeat, her light green eyes are on me, and then before too long, all I feel is a smile pushin' up my face. And it's funny, but I swear the world just stops, like literally, just freezes on its axis, just so we can have our moment—a private moment, where we say everything and nothin' at all. And I can't be sure what she's sayin', but I know what I'm sayin'. I'm sayin': I like you; I think you might like me, at least a little; and I don't want this conversation to end; and I, sure as hell, don't want this night to end. *And for just this moment, the chattering, the people, the smell of alcohol, of perfume, of the bonfire in the background— everything—disappears. And it's only us. And as I sit planted in this lawn chair, lookin' into her eyes, my heart starts this strange beat. I'm nervous and excited...and so damn nervous...and so damn excited, until suddenly, her eyes drop to my chest. And the moment's gone.*

"That's a nice jacket." She says the compliment evenly and without much expression. I find it a little out of character, but then again, what the hell do I know about her character, I guess? I just met her.

"Thanks," I say.

For a moment, it's almost as if she's in deep thought about somethin', and I want to know what it is, but I don't feel right askin' about it—just yet. So, instead, I change the subject. "So what do you do, Ashley Westcott?"

Her eyes slowly move up my chest and to my mouth and finally to my eyes. "Hmm?" she asks.

"What pays your bills, Miss Westcott?" I ask again. I'm smilin', but she's not.

"Oh." She seems to snap out of a trance of some sort. "Marijuana," she says, flatly.

You probably could have pushed me over with a feather at that.

"I'm kidding," she says, after a few heartbeats.

I let go of a long breath. I think I was more surprised than anything. "I deserved that."

She flashes me a triumphant smile. "I work at Sophia's Publishing House off of Elm Street in Fairfield. We publish children's books."

"Aah." I sit back further in my chair. "The creative type. They don't make many of those here."

Her face lights up a little more. "Well?"

"Well, what?" I ask.

"Well, what pays your *bills, Remington Jude?"*

"Oh," I say, sittin' up again, "I develop websites for companies, mostly smaller businesses, but I work with this guy who lives in Austin now. So, that's why I've gotta go down there every once in a while."

She nods, as if approvingly. "I see," she says.

I could be crazy, but I feel as if she keeps stealin' glances at me, like she's memorizin' every part of me or somethin'.

"So, where does a creative soul like yourself hail from?" I ask.

She bows her head. It looks as if she's turned a little shy all of a sudden. "Omaha."

"Aah, I think I've heard of it."

A soft laugh falls from her lips.

"Now, are we talkin' city-limits Omaha or rural Omaha?" I ask.

She raises her eyebrows. "We're talkin' the half-million-people-in-one-place Omaha."

"Oh," I say, scratchin' my stubble. "So, you mean the

Starbucks Omaha then?"

"Mm-hmm," she confirms.

"And the rush-hour Omaha?" I ask.

She nods again. "That's right."

"And the you-graduated-with-more-than-twenty-five-people-in-your-class Omaha."

"That's the one," she says.

"Well, this must be a far cry from what you're used to then."

She only smiles.

"So what brings you here?" I ask.

I watch her chest slowly rise with an intake of breath before she gradually pushes it out. "Well, I heard so much about this place that I wanted to see it for myself, I guess."

I don't know if I mean to, but I narrow my eyes at her. "This place?" I ask. "Are we talkin' about the same place?"

"Oh, come on, it's beautiful," she says, sittin' back and crossin' one leg over the other. "It's exactly how I pictured it—small town, America; apple festivals; hot air balloon races; maple trees lining the streets; everybody knows everybody."

"Wait," I say, reachin' for my phone in my pants pocket.

"What?" she asks, suddenly eyeing me a little closer. "What are you doing?" She gives me only half a grin.

"I'm gonna record this," I say, "for five years down the road when you've outgrown this place and you wanna get the hell out of here."

She laughs, and at the same time, swipes at my phone. Her skin brushes my skin, sending a hot sensation up my spine. "Really," she says, like she's tryin' to convince me. "I love it here."

"Okay," I reluctantly concede, putting my phone back into my pocket, but really, I'm just prayin' that she falls in love with me before she falls out of love with this place.

"So, you said you grew up here," she says. "I'm

guessing this is where you call home *then."*

"Yeah," I confirm. "That would be a pretty damn good guess."

She keeps her stare on me, and if eyes could smile, I'd have to say hers were smilin' right now.

"Ashley Westcott," a voice calls from the bottom of the porch steps. "I'm glad you found the place."

I look up and find Jack suddenly hoverin' over us. He winks at me and then slaps me on the back. Jack's always been a back-slapper. "My buddy here has been talkin' about ya nonstop since ya got into town."

She cocks her pretty blond head in my direction. "Has he?"

Before I can say anything...or knee Jack in the groin, he opens his big mouth again. "Yeah, he sure has. I had to invite everyone in Conoco just so it wouldn't seem like a stranger was askin' you to some backwoods party or somethin'. Hell, now I've got Old Crazy Kip runnin' around here lookin' for his whiskey and his cane just because he was buyin' an egg sandwich this mornin'."

She laughs. I try not to, especially since now I'm wonderin' where I'm gonna find Crazy Kip passed out in the mornin'.

"Anyway, Ashley, this here's a good guy. You should give him a chance." *He pats me on the back again and then leans over and whispers into her ear, loud enough that I can hear it.* "No pressure, but if ya don't, I might wind up a dead man tomorrow. I think somebody pissed on his garage door."

"What?" *I interject.*

Jack flaps his arms at me. "I'm just jokin'. It's just a joke." *He starts backin' away with his hands up in the air, but before he takes off, he whispers near her ear again.* "Don't take him by the garage door."

"Jack!" *I say, shaking my head.*

"Hey, at least you can watch the game on Saturday,"

he shouts back at me. "You know, instead of pushin' a grocery cart." He makes the motion of pushin' a cart, then disappears. And then it's just me and my reluctant smile and her questioning stare.

"Sorry about that," I say. "He's harmless." And before I can say anything else, I hear her soft voice.

"Your friends seem pretty cool."

I just keep one eye on her, while I pull out my phone again and look for the record button. "Can you repeat that, just one more time?"

She swipes at my hand, but this time, her touch lingers. And for a moment, I get lost in her light eyes.

"There's something about you, Remington Jude," she says in a low, velvety voice.

I don't say anything. I don't know if it's her touch or the way she says my name so soft and so sweet, but somethin's got me tongue-tied.

"Just like this town, there's something about you," she continues, barely over a whisper.

I don't know exactly what she's talkin' about, but I don't think I have to know either. All I hear is that she's stayin' here and that she likes me. At least, that's what I'm hopin' I'm hearin'. And that's all I need to know.

"Ashley Westcott, what are you doin' tomorrow night?"

She smiles, but it looks as if she tries to hide it by bowin' her head before lookin' back up at me. "I suppose you have an idea."

"Well, I might."

"Shoot," she says.

"Well, I was just wonderin' if I could borrow a little of your time."

Another beautiful smile breaks across her face.

"I mean," I go on, "just an afternoon...and maybe an evening." And hopefully, the rest her life too, but I'll keep that one to myself...for now.

She stares back at me—those pink lips holdin'

everything that keeps me breathin' right now.

"If a little time is all you're asking for," she says, "I suppose I can give that to you."

And with that, I sit back and smile because Jack and the garage door and Crazy Kip and the hell of a mess I know I'll have to clean up tomorrow mornin' all just became a part of what I know I'll remember as the best day of my crazy life...and also the day of no return.

I can't go back now. I've fallen for Ashley Westcott. And as of today, no matter what comes after this, I know I'll never be able to forget her. I know I'll never be able to forget the natural way her name hangs on my lips or the manner in which her beautiful green eyes can burrow a hole as deep as a silo into my soul. Not to mention, she gives a whole new meaning to a holey pair of jeans, an old, Cardinals tee shirt and cherry, red Chap Stick. And I'll be damned if this girl isn't the reason men don't move on from their first loves. In fact, I have no doubt that she broke a heart to get here. But hell, I'm just happy she's here, and better yet, that's she's givin' me a chance.

Chapter Six

Past

Rem

*F*or *the first ten times or so I came here, I hated it. My palms would get sweaty; my heart would damn near beat out of my chest; and my lungs would shrink to the size of marbles. But eventually, it got easier. It got better than easier, I guess. Somewhere along the line, it became... Oh, what's that damn word my mom always uses. Therapeutic. It became therapeutic-like, like I was just goin' to visit him, like it was just another day. And now, I guess, it's just like it's the two of us hangin' out and talkin' about the crazy shit in our lives—just like old times.*

I get to his spot. It's the one next to Mr. Katz. His is the stone stickin' out of the ground with the rounded edges. Most of the stones here are square and lie flat, including Mr. Katz's. But not Owen's. His is different than all the rest. It's even got a different color. Where all the others resemble limestone, his is more like sandstone—not quite gray, but not quite gold either. If I close my eyes, I can see it on the back of my eyelids, just like that. And even sometimes, right before I drift off to sleep, that gravestone is what I see. Owen Katz. Nov. 3, 1989 – Nov. 6, 2011. *And underneath that, I even see the football with his number—12—carved into it. So, whether I like it or not, this stone has become just as much a part of me as my own hand.*

I sit down on one of my grandpa's old milkin' stools I brought here about a year ago. I figured if I was gonna be spendin' some time here, I might as well pull up a chair.

"Hi, Mr. Katz." I tip my cap's bill in the direction of the stone that lies next to Owen's. It's a little older and a little more weathered around its square edges.

Mr. Katz—or Sam Katz—was Owen's dad. I never met him. He died of a heart attack right after Owen was born. I guess that should have been a red flag with Owen playin' football and all, but he seemed healthy. Nobody guessed there was anything wrong with Owen's heart—not until he went down in that last game, and he never got back up.

"Hey, buddy." I turn my attention back to the gray-gold stone.

I'm about to say somethin' else when my eye catches on somethin' other than the unopened can of beer Jack always leaves behind; that's how I always know he's been here. I reach for the other thing beside it. It's a postcard. On the front is a photo of a sunset over a beach. It reads Rio de Janeiro *in cursive letters at the bottom. I flip it over. The back is empty. It's always empty. I flip it back around and set it back where it was, against the stone. Every month or so, there's a new postcard. They started comin' not too long after he got here, about a couple years ago. The photos are always taken from exotic places like some South American beach or some jungle or desert somewhere; things like that. Owen never talked about places like that to any of us—not to* me, not to Jack, not to Mike. I didn't even know he knew about places like that. So, I figure whoever is leavin' these cards has got to be someone who talked to him more than we did. My guess is it's a girlfriend. He was always mysterious when it came to girls. Hell, he was always mysterious when it came to about everything. I just figured that since he lived most of his life in a small town where everybody always knew your business that the moment he got the chance, he disappeared. When he got that scholarship to play football up north, he moved up there, and I think he figured out real quick that if he never told anyone anything about his life up there that no one down here would ever have anything to say about him. He liked that. He liked when people kept to themselves and didn't bother with the rumor mill. And that's why, I suspect, that for those three and a half years he was away at school, we never heard a thing about a girlfriend.

My eyes travel from the stone to the postcard. I know that postcard is from someone who loved him, someone who knew more about him than his own friends and family. And there's a part of me that wished I knew who she was. I don't know what I'd say to her exactly. Maybe I'd just like to know from her what he was like up there. I'd guess he was a lot like he was here in Missouri. But then again, Missouri-Owen wouldn't understand a blank postcard of some sandy beach in Rio de Janeiro either.

I pick up the card again and look at it one more time. I just want to make sure I'm not missin' anything.

I flip it over. Nope. No name. No postmark. Nothin'.

"Owen, you ever gonna tell me who your girlfriend is?"

I laugh to myself and set the card back down.

"It's all right, buddy, you ain't gotta tell me. She seems like a nice girl, though. Looks like ya did pretty good."

I take a breath and then force it right back out, as I stare at that sandy beach on that card. "I guess you wanted to see the world, huh?"

I wait for him to answer, but all I hear is a squirrel

rustlin' some leaves in the tree next to us. I feel as if I wouldn't be startled if Owen actually did answer me, though. It would be just like him to scare the crap out of me—even from the grave.

"I'm sorry you never got to see your places," I say, lookin' at his name carved in that hard stone. "But then, I guess you got to see paradise before all the rest of us. And I suppose that's even better."

Chapter Seven

Past

"I *found another one of those postcards today," I say.*
Jack looks up at me with a puzzled face. In the
meantime, Kristen stops at our table and slides me and Jack
each a beer.

"Oh, at Owen's?" Jack asks, tippin' back the bill of his
cap.

Kristen instantly freezes up, and Jack and I both cringe.
"Sorry, Kristen," Jack says, averting his eyes from her.
If I would have known she was comin', I wouldn't have
said anything. Even just the mention of his name triggers
tears for Kristen. It always does. But I understand. We all
grew up together, and we all handle it differently, I guess.

Kristen swipes at her eyes with the back of her hand
and then quickly disappears without sayin' a word.

When I know she's out of earshot, I finally answer him. "Yeah," I say, takin' a swig from my bottle.

"You know," he says, "maybe it's Kristen." I notice his stare find her slender frame across the room. "She always kept one eye on him when we were kids."

Kristen's been waitressing here at Hall's through college. I've known her since we were in diapers. Jack's always had a thing for Kristen. Kristen's always had a thing for anyone but Jack, even though you'd never know it by watchin' 'em. And I don't think she had a thing for Owen, but then I didn't know Owen had a thing for anyone, either.

"And it would explain all those mysterious trips she used to take," he adds.

"She was visiting her grandma in Florida," I say.

"Well," he says, still lookin' over at her. "That's what she says anyway." His eyes eventually wander back over to me, and he points the neck of his bottle in my direction. "And that would also explain why she doesn't even bat an eye at you, like every other girl in this damn town. She's still in love with him."

Jack looks disgusted, but I know he's okay. Girls like him all right, too. And he knows it.

I smile, but I let out a sigh at the same time and glance over at Kristen. "We would have known, right? If they had a thing or somethin'?"

He shrugs one shoulder. "I don't know. You know how he got all secretive—more than he already was—when he went off to college. Who the hell knows?"

I breathe in a weighted breath and then push it right back out again, feelin' that constant sense of loss that Owen left behind.

"Hey, buddy," he says, focusin' all his attention on me now. "We all miss him."

I nod. "Yeah," I say. "I know."

"Only the good die young." He raises his bottle in the air.

Without another thought, I raise mine too. "That's for damn sure," I add.

Chapter Eight

Present

Rem

The airport is crowded for a Tuesday. I wonder for a second where in the hell all these people are goin'.

I find my gate and take a seat in between an old man who's mastered the art of sleeping sittin' up in a chair and a younger girl, maybe in junior high, cradlin' her phone in both hands. I stare at her hands for a second longer than I normally would have. I've just never seen anyone move their thumbs so fast. They're like Riverdance thumbs or somethin'.

Just then, her thumbs stop movin', and I look away. Luckily, I don't think she noticed me starin'. It's either that or she doesn't care because she never takes her eyes off the phone.

The electric board above the little ticket counter distracts me by changing to a different set of numbers. I glance down at my boarding pass. The flight number on the board matches the one on my pass. *Right on time.* I like to cut things close. I hate sittin' and waitin'. I'd rather miss the damn flight than sit here hours waitin' for it.

A moment later, a woman's voice comes over the speakers. She tells us they're startin' to board. So, like my grandpa's cattle ready to feed, myself included, we all get up and shuffle to the line that's already formin' behind that ticket counter. I'm there for all of two seconds before somethin' hits my leg. And without even so much as a thought, I turn around and catch a young blonde bendin' down. She's grabbin' at the handle of the bag that just fell and hit me. And in an attempt to help her, I bend down and reach for the bag as well.

"I'm so sorry," she says, in a rushed voice.

At her words, my heart starts to panic, and I lose all my thoughts. And I just stand there, waiting—waiting to see her face—even though, I already know who I'm about to see.

One Mississippi.

My heart's about ready to beat out of my chest.

Two Mississippi.

The seconds feel like years. And meanwhile, I can't get a breath.

Three Mississippi.

Our eyes meet, and she gasps.

"Rem."

I can't tell if it's a statement or a question. And I'm so dumbstruck, I can't even command my lips to move.

She steadies the bag upright again and crosses her arms in front of her chest. "Um...uh... Hi."

It takes me a second, but I eventually get the word

out. "Hi."

One Mississippi.

Two Mississippi.

"Uh, how have you been?" She asks it sincerely, as if she really means it. I think that hurts more than anything.

I breathe in first. I don't think I had done that in a few seconds. And then, thankfully, I breathe out a smile. "I'm good." I nod. "You?"

She nods too. "Good," she says.

There's this breathless silence and a look between us that lasts a little too long. And if that's not enough, my heart tries to climb up my throat, but I do my best to swallow it down.

"Well," she says, droppin' her gaze, and at the same time, fiddlin' with the jacket she has in her hands. "Meeting?" she asks, looking up and at the board that reads *Austin*.

"Yeah," I simply say.

She nods, as if she expected my answer.

It's funny. I did picture seeing her again. I did. There were those moments in the day when it was really quiet and then at night, when the world seemed asleep, that I pictured how this exact moment would play out. It was always in a crowded place. She would see me, and I would see her, and then the world around us would stop and fall away, like loose tiles on a wall. And it would always be as if we were expecting to see each other—as if we knew at any point, in any given day, that we would meet again, that it was inevitable. We just didn't know when. And when we'd see each other for the first time in ages, our eyes would meet, and it would be as if all the pain were gone—as if *it* never happened. And she would smile. And I would smile. And we would reminisce about the first day we met or that night in Sunny Square. And then...and then, we'd look into each other's eyes, and we'd promise each other, without sayin' a word, that we'd make it...this time.

It's funny now, though. There's still a tinge of pain, and in place of that happy feelin' I always pictured I'd have, there's this huge hole of speechlessness and uncertainty. And *work*... In all the dreams, *work* was never a topic that came up.

"You?" I ask. "Why are you headed down south?"

"I...I live in Lakeway now. It's not too far from Austin. I figured, I could work and keep tabs on my grandmother." She bows her head and softly laughs. "Though, I think she's actually the one keeping tabs on me."

I smile, but somethin' in my chest jabs at my heart. I don't know why, but the fact that she lives in Texas now kind of hits me hard. I think it's because it's the first time I realize that I'm really no longer a part of her life. I didn't even know where she lived.

"I was just here visiting some friends," she adds.

That hurts too. I'm not even a friend she'd consider visiting. And I don't even know if I'd know the friends she was visiting. Her friends used to be our friends, but then, I guess, you can make all new friends in the course of a year.

I nod.

"Are you still in Ava?" she asks.

"Yeah," I say, grabbin' the back of my neck. I think it's a nervous habit.

She takes a deep breath. "How is everyone?"

Again, she asks it as if she really cares. Why does she have to ask it that way? I'm tryin' not to picture her against that old maple, lookin' into my eyes, smilin' that pretty smile of hers and tellin' me she loves me. And her being nice isn't helpin' any.

The line starts movin', and all of a sudden, I notice there's a gap between me and the person in front of me. Ashley smiles and rests her hand on the handle of her bag. I take that as a cue and shuffle up the line sideways a couple more feet.

"Everyone's fine," I say. "I'm sure they're all the same as when you left."

I notice her draw a sharp breath at my last word. I didn't mean to make her hurt, but the fact is, she did leave—fast. Nobody leaves where I'm from, and they sure as hell don't do anything fast. But then, I guess, I might have left—fast—too, if I were her.

All too soon, I'm bein' stared at by a tall, slender woman takin' tickets. She gives me a rushed smile, so I make an effort to smile, too, as I hand her my pass. She takes it, scans it, and I slowly shuffle into the tunnel that leads to the plane. But I stop when the line stops and watch as Ashley hands her ticket over and eventually joins me in the tunnel.

"You packed light," she says, crossing her arms over her chest.

I look down at the backpack I'm corralling at the end of my fingertips. "I try to avoid baggage claim at all costs these days."

She lowers her head and smiles. "Me too."

I inhale and eye her one little carry-on. Today, I wouldn't mind a stay in baggage claim if she were goin' to be there. *Damn, I really shouldn't be thinkin' these thoughts anymore.*

"What seat are you?" she asks.

For the first time, I look to see my seat assignment. Until now, I didn't care where I sat.

"15C," I say.

"I think I'm in 11." She looks down at her ticket. "11A."

She looks up at me then. There's something in her eyes. There's somethin' she's not sayin'. And more than anything right now, I want to know what that somethin' is.

"You know, if there's an empty seat...you should sit next to me," she says. Her words are soft and unsure.

I nod and start to smile. "I could do that."

She presses her lips together, while I say a little prayer that the seat next to her isn't taken.

"It's been a long time," she says, bringin' me back to the moment.

My eyes land on hers. She smiles.

"Yeah," I agree. I take a deep breath. "You still workin' in publishing?"

She nods. "Yeah. I am. But I'm writing, too." She grins a little wider now.

"Really?" I ask.

"Yeah." She fidgets with her jacket. "Well, a little."

"Wow," I say. I'm a little surprised at how genuinely excited I am for her. "That's really cool."

All too soon, we're at the door to the plane, and the flight attendant is starin' me down. I shuffle into the tiny aisle and immediately notice how full the plane is already. *Eight. Nine. Ten. Eleven. Damn it!* There's already two guys sittin' in Ashley's row. I give them a good once over. They're about our age—two young city boys. I'm instantly jealous, and I'm not exactly sure why. She's not mine...anymore. But even so, I size 'em up and figure pretty quickly that I could probably take 'em. Knowin' that makes me feel a little better.

I stay back to help Ashley get her bag into the overhead compartment, even though she really doesn't need my help. I try to act casual about the whole thing, and I make damn sure I make eye contact with each of the city boys at least once. They don't need to know she's not mine.

"Thanks," she says.

I nod.

"Well," she says, lookin' over at her seat, "in case I don't see you when we get off..."

She stops. And there's somethin'. There's somethin' there again. I should say somethin'. I should ask her to lunch or...

Another guy about our age in line behind us loudly clears his throat and cuts short my thoughts. I give him a stern look.

"Well, if I don't see you later," she starts over, "it was nice seeing you again, Rem."

I almost say somethin', but then I don't. "Yeah," I say, instead. "Yeah, it was nice to see you, too."

She smiles, turns and then takes her seat. And after another long breath, I drag my feet to my seat and plop down next to two people—a woman and a child. And I just sit there and stare into the back of the seat in front of me, thinkin' about what just happened. I just saw Ashley Westcott for the first time in more than a year, and she's just as beautiful as the day I met her. And I still want her just as much, yet there's that wall there. She knows it's still there; I know it's still there. It's keepin' me from sayin' anything. And I know it's keepin' her from sayin' anything, too.

I try my best to see her through the cracks in the seats, but I can't, and after several more minutes, I eventually give up. And then gradually, my mind goes back to the last couple years. I think about the time we were together and the time we were apart. I think about our first dance and our last day together. And I stop there. And I kick myself for not sayin' more to her just now. But then I feel my heart drop in my chest when I realize that no matter what I could have said today, the outcome still remains the same.

And before I can even imagine that much time goin' by, an hour and forty-five minutes is gone. And right on time, the voice comes over the speakers tellin' us to buckle our seatbelts and make sure our seat backs and tray tables are in their full, upright positions. I glance out the window and see the tops of buildings. *Had we really been up in the air for nearly two hours already?*

I do as the voice commands, and then I just sit there and think about her some more. I don't know if I'm gonna see her again once I get off this plane. I want to see her, but then, it might be easier if I don't.

The plane takes its good ol' time taxiing to a gate and then finally opens its doors. And as if someone literally gives the word—although, no one ever does—a dozen rows of people stand up in front of me. Usually, I stay sittin'. I've learned it doesn't do me any good to start rushin' too soon. I liken people gettin' off of a plane to a herd of turtles crossin' the road. But today is different. Today, my palms are sweaty, and my heart is racin'. And it's all because of a girl—a girl I never quite got over. And I've gotta do whatever it takes to see her one more time—even if I have no idea what to do after that.

I stand and look for her, but I can't see her through all the damn heads swayin' back and forth. So, I grab my backpack and just wait. I wait for enough people to crawl off the plane before I follow the line between the two rows of seats. I notice her seat is empty when I pass it. I tip my cap to thank the flight attendants and make my way into the tunnel. I hurry through it, and within seconds, I'm at the gate. I look up and immediately see her bent over a chair, messin' with her bag. My heart instantly speeds up a notch, and I smile.

She could have stalled on purpose. She could have just needed somethin' out of her carry-on. Either way, I'm happy to see her. I take a few moments just to watch her. There was a time I called her *mine*. I used to be able to walk up behind her and put my arms around her waist and kiss the soft skin on the back of her neck. I used to be the only man in the world that could get away with doin' that.

I used to be.

Those are the four saddest words in the English language, according to my grandpa. And it's not until just this very moment that I understand why.

I feel my smile startin' to fade the moment I realize that *that* time is gone now. And after a few more seconds of me starin' at her, not exactly knowin' what to do next, she finishes what she's doin' and looks up. Immediately, our eyes meet, and she smiles. I feel the hesitation in my bones. It's as if there's this disconnect between my mind and my feet, all of a sudden. I want to go to her, but I can't, and she knows it. I see the hesitation in her eyes, too, and it kills me.

One Mississippi.

Two Mississippi.

I can't look away from her, even as her happy smile turns sad and falls from her pink lips.

And then she waves.

It's just a simple, subtle wave, but it holds a word I've grown to hate. *Good-bye.*

I force myself to keep it together, as I manage to lift my arm, open my hand and muster a small smile. She gives me this knowing look, and then she turns.

And she walks away.

And I just stand there for a few moments, watchin' her, watchin' her walk away. And the whole time, my heart is screamin' at my mind—tellin' me to chase after her—but it's not doin' any damn good. My feet stay planted exactly where they are, until eventually, I can't see her blond hair anymore. And it's not until then that I take a step after her.

But then I stop.

And just like that, the world comes to a halt. Everything's at a standstill—except my heart. It keeps beatin' a hole into my chest, tearin' right through every bone and muscle fiber I've got tryin' to protect it. It beats like that until I draw in a long, deep breath, and then I feel it eventually startin' to slow. And after a few more telling moments, I mindlessly sling my backpack over my shoulder and start my walk in the opposite direction.

It was just like the movies. I don't look back. I'll never know if she does. And that's it. The love of my life comes back into my life for exactly one hour and forty-five minutes, and it's nothin' how I expected it would be. Nowhere even close. Yet, it's exactly as it should be. It's exactly as it needs to be.

Chapter Nine

Past (2 Years Earlier)

Rem

"**S**o, this is it," I say, spreading my arms wide. "The Times Square of Ava. I know all the lights and fanfare are probably burnin' your eyes. Just try not to look at it all at once."

She gives me a sweet smile.

It's our first date. I'm nervous as hell, but she seems as cool as the other side of the pillow. I wish I had some of her courage.

I look over at a crowd gatherin' around the stand that sells grilled hot dogs and cheap beer. "Can I tell you somethin' you probably already know?" I ask.

She looks up at me. "Sure."

"All right, well, this right here," I say, pointin' to the ground at our feet, "is quite possibly the *only place to be on a Friday evening in Ava."*

She nods. "Somehow, I gathered that." Her eyes wander over the crowd. "Is everyone here?"

"Just about," I say, takin' in all the people and the street vendors and the lights that line the walkway. We're downtown. Everyone calls it Sunny Square. Most people don't know why it's called that, but I do. My grandma told me why years ago.

"Can I tell you somethin' you probably don't already know?"

"Sure," she agrees once more, showin' off her teeth this time.

"This place got its name years ago, back when the farmers market was goin' on down here and they used to play matinées at the theater." I point in the direction of the big glass doors framed in oak with the black and white marquee hangin' above them. "You wouldn't know it now because it's gettin' dark, but this is the sunny side of the block by early afternoon. Hence, Sunny Square."

It looks as if she tries not to laugh. "That sounds very...logical."

"Well, we're a simple people, Miss Westcott."

She bows her head and just nods as we continue our walk down the sidewalk, passin' by Joe Kimper sellin' his county-famous kettle corn.

"Wait, you've gotta try this," I say, backin' up and stoppin' at the stand. "Can I have a bag, Joe?"

He nods and hands me a long, white paper sleeve. I immediately offer some to her, and she obliges.

"So, I know your name and where you're from," I go on. "And I know you showed up here a few months ago. And I know you're pretty as hell, but I don't know anything else about you."

She raises her head just a little, just enough that she's lookin' up at me through her dark eyelashes. I'd swear she was tryin' to hide the little blush on her cheeks. "Well, what do you want to know?"

She puts some of the kettle corn to her mouth, and for a moment, my stare is stuck on her pretty, pink lips.

"Everything," I say to her.

"Everything?"

"Yep," I agree with a nod. "I want to know you better than I know this town."

"Hmm," she hums. "I'm guessing that would be everything then, all right."

"Pretty much," I agree.

She puts another handful of kettle corn to her mouth.

"Well, I can tell you I love this popcorn."

I just smile wide. I knew she would.

She giggles then and quickly covers her mouth. It looks as if she's tryin' to keep the food from spillin' out.

"Okay," I say, tryin' not to laugh, "so what about...your favorite childhood memory then?"

"My what?" She swallows and reaches into the white sleeve again.

"Your favorite memory—like the one that defines your childhood. You know? The one memory you couldn't make leave your head, even if you tried."

She eyes me, and at the same time, pushes her lips to one side. "That sounds like a lot of pressure."

I just shrug my shoulders, offering her no escape. In response, she tilts her head back and looks up into the darkening sky before levelin' her eyes back on me. "Does everyone have one of these?"

"They sure do," I say with a definitive nod. "You can tell a lot about a person by the memories they hold dear."

"Can you now?"

I laugh. "Well, that's what my grandma always used to say."

"Okay," she concedes. "Um, well..." Her gaze wanders to the ground for a few seconds. "Okay. When we were growing up, we had this old house, like turn-of-the-century

kind of old." She pauses. "Like the last century. Not this one."

"I gotcha," I say. "Like horse-and-buggy old, not Y2K."

She looks at me and smiles. "Right," she agrees, "like that. And anyway," she goes on, "the house had a furnace room. It was just this little room with this big, scary gray box that would kick on with this loud bang every time the heat would come on. But the room was so warm in the winter, and my sister and I would always huddle in the corner next to the big box. It was like our secret hiding place. We would sneak back there when no one was looking, and we'd eat frosted flakes out of the box." She stops and laughs. Her eyes are trained on somethin' out in front of us, but it looks as if she's more interested in seein' the memory than whatever it is her eyes are stuck on.

"Frosted flakes?" I ask.

"Yeah," she says. "My mom hated when we ate the cereal straight out of the box. We thought we were such rebels."

I smile because she looks so happy and because I like her memory.

"Well?" she asks.

"Well, what?"

"Well, what does that tell you about me?"

"Oh," I say. "Well... You like your sister—well, enough to share a box of frosted flakes with her. ...And you're tough." I stop there because she's givin' me a funny look.

"Tough?"

"Yeah, you weren't afraid of the big, scary furnace."

"Aah," she says, with a smile.

"And...you've got a little of a wild streak in ya."

She laughs. "So, it all started with those frosted flakes."

I look at her with raised brows. "I wouldn't doubt it."

We both laugh this time.

"Well, what about you?" she asks. "What's your

favorite memory?"

I suck in a deep breath. "Well," I say, forcin' the breath back out. "Every spring, my dad and I would go mushroom huntin'."

She gives me a questionin' stare, and I figure I've probably gotta explain a little more.

"Morels."

She's still givin' me that confused look.

"You've never had one?"

She shakes her head, and little wrinkles form above her nose and on her forehead. "No, I can't say I have."

"Oh, well, city girl, you need to add fried morel sandwiches to your bucket list. You won't be sorry."

She laughs. "Okay, I'll look for them next time I'm at the grocery store."

I look at her to see if she's joking.

"What?" she asks.

"No, sweetheart, you don't get these from the grocery store. You've gotta find 'em."

"Find them?" She looks sincerely surprised.

"Yeah, but don't worry, I'll take you sometime."

There's a slight pause in her expression, but then, thankfully, she smiles and holds her stare on me. I swear her eyes could kill a man, if he weren't strong enough to take the hit to his heart.

"But anyway, we would spend hours lookin' for 'em," I go on. "I really can't remember anything specific we talked about. I just remember bein' with them, and that might as well have been the best thing in the world."

"Them?"

"What?"

"You said you remember being with them.*"*

"Oh." I try to recall it for a second. "Did I say that?" She looks at me and just nods.

"I meant my dad." I shrug it off. "I remember being with my dad."

"Oh, so you guys are pretty close then—you and your dad?"

"Yeah," I say, givin' her a quick nod. "He's a pretty good dad."

I catch her eyes and stay in them for a second or two as our conversation grows quiet. I don't know why or how, but the way she's lookin' at me makes me feel good. And I'm also pretty sure that's what's causing these thoughts of kissin' her lips to pop into my head, all of a sudden.

"Okay," she says. "How did you get into the website business?"

I take a moment to gather my thoughts, but mostly, I just stall so I can get my mind off of kissin' her and back to our conversation. "Well," I finally say, barely noticin' that we're now roundin' the corner of the block. "I've always kind of been fascinated with computers. I got my associate's at a small college here and started a company with a buddy I knew in high school. He has a few small clients in Austin. I have some here. It's worked thus far."

"Really?" She sounds sincerely interested. "That's pretty cool."

I always think the whole computer-job-spiel thing makes me look like a dork. Around here, you farm, work in construction or find somethin' else to do with your hands. And computers ain't one of those things. In fact, just the other day, I ran into the town mechanic, a guy who's been around long enough to tell ya what kind of car your grandpa drove before he met your grandma. Anyway, he asked me what I was doin' these days. I told him I work in computers. And he just leaned back on his heels, narrowed his eyes, put an oil-stained finger to his wrinkled chin and said: "Well, that there's some fancy job." I just smiled. I wanted to tell him I could replace a carburetor if I had to, but I figured he'd already made up his mind. I was fancy, and that was that.

I squint one eye at her. "You did hear the computer-

nerd part?"

She laughs. Her laugh is breathy and honest. I think I just fell in love with it, or hell, maybe I just fell in love with her.

"I don't think computers make people nerds anymore," she says, her lips pushed to one side.

"Really?"

"Really," she confirms.

"Could you tell that to the guy behind the counter at Hochman Mechanics?"

"What?"

"Nothin'," I say, laughin' to myself.

Our eyes lock then, and we're both silent for a few beats. Her eyes are beautiful. They're soft and curious. Everything about them—about her—makes me want to kiss her even more.

"And anyway," she says, "you're so young, and you own a business. That's pretty impressive."

"Well," I say, tryin' to regain my bearings. "I'm not that young." I notice her hand, and I really want to take it, but I don't. "You know Steve Jobs?"

"Yeah?"

"He was twenty-one when he started Apple." I point one finger in the air. "And William Harley..."

"The motorcycle guy?"

"Yep. He was twenty-one, too, when he drew up the plans for the first bicycle motor. So, you see, twenty-one's not all that young."

She stops and stares me down for a second. "Wait, so are you...?"

I hesitate before I say my next words. "I just turned twenty-one a month ago."

It takes her a second, but then she nods.

"Too young? Too old?" I ask.

"No, I just...," she stutters. "With the company and the house... You seemed older, that's all."

"Oh," I say. "That's just my real age—the one you could figure out by lookin' at my driver's license. I'm older in small-town age."

"Small-town age?" She barely gets the words out through her giggles.

"Yeah, people in small towns age a little faster than big-city folk."

"I'm scared to ask why that is."

And she does look a little scared, but also, a little intrigued.

"Oh, it's simple really," I say. "We just do everything earlier out of necessity. We drive younger; we work younger; we drink younger. I guess it all comes down to work really."

"Work?" She's got this little, challenging smile on her face. I wonder if she knows it's drivin' me wild.

"Yeah," I say. "For example, in order to help my grandpa out on the farm when I turned thirteen, I had to learn how to drive. And after a long day of workin' in the field, all I wanted was a cold soda. But Grandpa only ever had cold beer. So, I had my first beer at thirteen, and no one even batted an eye. In fact, my grandpa came into the kitchen right after me, grabbed his own beer from the fridge and sat down across from me, and we had some conversation about Grandma makin' pork chops and mashed potatoes for dinner." I shrug. "And so you see, I'm really more like twenty-three or twenty-four, when you think about it."

She doesn't say anything at first, but somehow I can tell her smile is sincere, and maybe it's because her eyes are as bright as that dusk-to-dawn light we just passed. "Wow, that explains it then," she eventually says, right before another pause. "I graduated from the University of Minnesota this past spring..."

"The University of Minnesota, huh?"

"Yeah," she says.

I try to swallow.

"I'm twenty-three," she says.

"Well," I say, clearin' my throat. "I can assure you, I'm the oldest twenty-one-year-old you'll ever meet."

She laughs and elbows my arm. I don't miss the fact that she touches me—even if it was just her elbow.

"We'll see about that," she says, givin' me another challengin' smile.

I love that smile. God, I love that smile.

We walk a few more steps, side by side, and then all of a sudden, she stops.

"What?" I ask.

"Bamboo plants," she says.

I look in the direction she's lookin'. Rose Darren has been sellin' these funny-lookin' plants for decades here. There are rumors that her house is lined wall to wall with the things and that she even put the ashes of her late husband in one of the plants she sleeps with every night. But I can neither confirm nor deny the rumors because, honestly, when you hear that story as a kid, you tend to keep your distance. Hell, I didn't even know what the funny-lookin' things were called until just now.

I watch Ashley walk over to the stand and focus first on a plant with two long, green stems juttin' out of a glass jar.

"Two stalks mean love...and luck," she says.

I walk closer to her and give the plant a funny look. I always thought they looked like pigs' tails the way they curl at their ends. Love or luck never came to mind.

I watch her as she moves over to a jar with three long, green stems stickin' out of it next. And without even knowin' I'm doin' it, I memorize the way she gently brushes her fingertips over each stem. There's a certain awe and tenderness in her movements. I've never seen anybody treat a plant that way. And I know it might sound crazy, but just like that, I gain this new admiration for her.

"Three stalks mean happiness, a long life and wealth,"

she says, draggin' me out of my thoughts.

I look up at her expression now. It's soft and thoughtful.
"How do you know all this stuff?"

She runs her fingers over the little leaves of the plant.
"My grandmother loves these things. She knows what each
one means." She pauses on a leaf and then takes her hand
back. "Every number of stalks means something different."

I nod and smile, and at the same time, make eye contact
with Rose, who's sittin' behind the wall of plants. She's in a
lawn chair, knittin' something long and blue. She pretends to
be a bystander to our conversation, but I know she's secretly
listenin'. I notice her look up and smile every once in a
while. And I notice somethin' else, too: She's not nearly as
scary as my eight-year-old mind made her out to be.

"I like the two stalks, I think," Ashley says. "I mean,
what good is a long life and wealth if you don't have love?"

She looks up at me with the question still hangin' in her
eyes.

"Good point," I say. "We'll take the jar with the
two...uh..."

"Bamboo stalks," Ashley says, finishin' my sentence,
thankfully.

I reach for my wallet in my back pocket.

"No," she says, touchin' her hand to my arm. "You
don't have to get it."

"But I want to," I assure her.

I pull out a bill and hand it to Rose. "Plus, Rose would
have never let me get away with lettin' you pay for a love
plant." I give Rose a wink.

"That is true," Rose says. The gray-haired woman
gives me a stern look, but it's quickly followed by an
approving smile. And the smile doesn't go unnoticed as I
pick up the jar and hand the plant to Ashley.

"Your love plant," I say.

"Thank you," she says, taking the plant. She looks
happy. I hope she is.

We continue walkin' then, until we reach the park bench on the other side of Sunny Square, aptly named Shady Park, a few minutes later. The bench sits right on top of the levee and overlooks the river. It's dark now, and without lights, it's even darker on this side of the block. In fact, until my eyes adjusted, I couldn't even see my own hand right in front of my face. But now, after a few moments, everything's a little clearer.

I take a seat, and she does too, as my eye catches on her love plant she's settin' on the ground at our feet.

I smile, then I look up and see the stars are poppin' out of the black sky now, and below, the water is flowin' like thick, dark oil inside the river's banks.

"So, what was your major?" I ask, lookin' over at her.

"Literature," she says, findin' my eyes before returnin' her gaze to the river.

"That makes sense—the children's books."

"Yeah," she agrees.

"So you like it—what you do?" I ask.

She hesitates for a moment. "Yeah," she says, noddin' her head. "Yeah, I do...for now."

I look over at her. "Then what? What big dreams do you have up your sleeve, Ashley Westcott?"

"Well..." I think I notice her inhale a little. "Someday, I'd like to write a book."

"A children's book?"

"Maybe...or maybe one for grown-ups. But that's a long way off."

"A novel?"

She just smiles.

"Wow, that's some big stuff, Miss Westcott." I look out onto the black water, takin' in the way the tiny waves break, pickin' up what little light there is to pick up from the moon and the stars. "The most I've ever written was a letter to my mom when I was in the second grade. It was a five-page dissertation on why I needed a dirt bike."

She laughs. "Did it work?"

"No," I say, lowerin' my head. I listen as her voice continues to hitch in soft laughter.

"But you know," I say, memorizing the way her laugh sounds to my ears, "it doesn't have to be...a long way off? You could start your novel now, right?"

Her smile grows a little wider. She almost looks giddy, like her heart is just plain full. "Well, I don't exactly have a story, yet."

I nod. "Well, I suppose someday you will."

"I hope so," she says, lookin' as if that dream is just plastered right on her eyelids, just out of reach.

"Come here," I say, gesturing her closer to me. I don't know where the bravery comes from all of a sudden. In that moment, she just looked so happy, so beautiful, so full of life; I couldn't help but have her nearer to me.

She eyes me hesitantly.

"Come on," I say, noticin' her pause. "It's only a limited-time offer. You refuse now, I'll have to leave the offer open indefinitely, and then my credibility will be shot to hell."

She looks as if she tries not to laugh right before she closes the gap between us. And when I feel her warm body press up against mine, I put my arm around her bare shoulder and squeeze her even closer. This feels right. In fact, this feels better than right.

"What about you?" She looks up at me with a playful, little look.

"What about me?" I ask.

"Oh, come on, Remington Jude, I know you dream. I can see it in your eyes."

I laugh. "In my eyes, huh?"

"Mm-hmm," she says. "You ain't foolin' a soul."

I look down at her nestled in the crook of my arm. "Where did that sweet, little small-town accent come from?"

She lifts a shoulder. "I don't know. Maybe it just comes

with the territory."

"Aah, I see." I feel myself chuckle a little more.

"Now, tell me your dreams, small-town boy," she demands.

"All right," I say, a smile playin' on my face. She settles into my arm, and I take a second to gaze out onto the river. "I think I want to travel. I've been thinkin' about it a lot lately. I've been here my whole life, and besides Austin, I haven't really seen too much. I've got these pictures...in my mind...of places I want to go. And I figure if I get to see even one of them in this life, I'd be pretty darn happy."

She glances up at me with a pair of warm eyes, and it's almost as if she gets lost there for a moment.

"What?" I ask. "It's a stupid dream, isn't it? I know it's not about a career or anything. But I'm already happy doin' what I do..."

"No," she says, stopping me short. "I think that's a nice dream." She says her last word and then rests her hand on mine.

My gaze falls to our hands. The feel of her skin touchin' mine makes me forget about everything but her touch. And slowly, my stare wanders back to her beautiful light eyes. And that private moment passes between us again. I like you. I think you like me. I want you, and I think you want me, too. I don't want this moment to end.

And then, without another thought, my lips are moving toward hers. And it's as if my world just breaks open when our lips touch. I close my eyes, and I can't think of anything better than kissing her, until she kisses me back, and then I can't think of anything better than her kissing me back. Her lips are soft, and her kiss is hungry. I just want more of her. I take my arm from around her shoulders, and I gently touch my fingertips to her suntanned face. And she kisses me like I've never been kissed before. She kisses me like she knows me, even though this is our very first kiss and we've only really known each other for a week. It's comfortable but also new and exciting, and I'm findin' out fast that I just can't get enough of her. I just can't get enough of the sweet taste of her lips and the way her mouth moves along mine. It's sexy and so damn addictive. But before too long, I need a breath. I try to fight it. I try to fight it with everything I have in me. But in the end, nature wins, and after a few lightning-fast moments, our kiss breaks.

I lean my forehead against hers. I'm smilin', and I can hear my breathing. "Ashley Westcott," I manage to get out, "you're one hell of a kisser."

I can feel the breaths from her soft laugh hit my lips.

"It must be part of my wild side," she whispers, her siren-like voice slowly pullin' me more and more in.

God, I want this girl so bad.

"It must be," I say, laughin' under my breath. "That frosted-flake lifestyle really did you in."

I can't see it, but I'm almost certain a playful smile fights its way to her mouth. "I guess it did," she softly confesses.

She keeps her forehead pressed against mine for a few more seconds, and then she pulls away slightly, and her green-eyed stare carefully wanders back into my eyes.

"Don't worry," I whisper, "your secret's safe with me."

Chapter Ten

Present

Rem

The guys are over. The game's about to start. This time, Mike went to get the cheeseburgers from Hall's, and he's not back yet, but Jack's sitting on the couch playin' with his phone, and I'm in my chair.

"I saw her," I say, barely over a mumble. I'm not sure yet if I want him to hear it. I just know I need to say it.

He doesn't look up. It doesn't even look as if he heard me. I sit back in my chair and breathe a little sigh of relief. I said it. That's all that matters.

"Wait." Jack lowers his phone and looks up at me. "What did you say?"

His hawk-like stare makes me straighten up. "What?"

He cocks one of his eyebrows up and gives me a puzzled look. "You just said something."

I shake my head. "No, I didn't."

"Yeah, you just said that you saw her."

"Nah." I shake my head. "You're hearin' things again."

He narrows an eye at me. "First off, I don't have a habit of hearin' things. Second, damn it, I'm not deaf. What do you mean you saw her?"

"Damn it," I push out, under my breath. "I saw her in the airport."

"When?"

"When I was in the airport," I say.

"Damn it, Rem!"

I laugh and run my hand along my thigh. "In St. Louis. She lives in Texas now."

"Texas?"

"Yeah," I confirm.

"Well, what'd she look like? What'd you say?"

"She looked...the same. And I didn't really say too much. In fact, I really didn't say anything at all."

Jack sets his phone onto the cardboard coffee table and sits back in the couch. "Wow," he says, his gaze straight ahead. He's got this laser-like focus on the wall, all of a sudden. "All this time, and then boom, there she is."

I nod my head. "Yeah, I know."

"She was like a missing person."

I nod again.

"So, she didn't say anything about... You know?"

I drag in a long breath and then shake my head. I know what he's gettin' at. "No," I finally say. "Nothin'."

"Really? She never said nothin' about why she left?"

"No," I say. "Nothin'."

60

"And you didn't...?"

"Bring it up?" I ask.

He just blankly stares back at me.

"No, surprisingly, in the few minutes we talked, that subject never came up."

"Well, I don't know," he says, shruggin' one shoulder. "I was just askin'."

I refit my cap over my head and catch myself starin' in the direction of the TV. I think I'm secretly hopin' it will distract me, or better yet, teleport me out of this room.

Jack is quiet. I don't say anything either. I had waited until Mike was gone before I said anything in the first place, mostly because Jack is the only one who'd really care to hear about it. But now, I don't really feel like talkin' about it anymore.

"Well, damn." He exhales or sighs or somethin', and I watch as he grabs his beer off the box. "I bet that was like seein' a ghost."

I smile halfheartedly. "Yeah, it kind of was."

"You all right?"

He gives me that same look he always gives me in situations like this. I've seen it at least a hundred times. We were seven when I got my first wild pitch—right to the eye. It turned black and blue on the spot. And I could tell he wanted to cry more than I did; but he didn't. He just stared at me in my one good eye, gave me that look and asked: "You all right?"

I shift in my chair a little. "Yeah," I say. "Yeah, I'm fine."

He takes a swig from the bottle and then swallows. "Well, is she still, uh...doin' the publishing thing?"

"She's actually writing now, evidently," I say.

"Ha!" He starts to laugh. "You better watch out. She

might end up writin' you into one of her stories."

I laugh to myself and sit deeper in my chair. "As long as she gives me better-lookin' friends in the fiction version."

Jack fishes a plastic soda bottle off the table box and throws it at me. "Shit, I ain't so bad on the eyes."

I deflect the bottle, and it goes flyin' to the floor. Good thing it was plastic.

"Now, Mike," Jack goes on, pointin' the neck of his bottle in my direction. "Mike could use some groomin'."

We both laugh just as Mike barrels down the stairwell, his long, shaggy hair trailin' behind him. He thinks his mane, along with the beard that goes with it, is what attracts the women. Jack and I think he's full of shit. But then again, there always seems to be a girl on his arm, so maybe he ain't as full of it as we think he is.

"Got your food, suckers." Mike drops the bag onto the box, pulls out a burger wrapped in white paper and falls into his usual chair in the corner.

"What'd I miss?" he asks, stuffin' half the burger into his mouth.

"Nothin'," I say, "it hasn't started yet."

"Well, what are you two Twinkies laughin' at then?"

Jack looks at me and then back at Mike.

"Oh, Rem, here, was just complimentin' us on how good we look."

Mike raises a brow at me, and at the same time, tugs at his beard. "About time you noticed. I told you it'd drive 'em crazy. Hell, even my dog likes me better this way."

Jack gives Mike a puzzled look before he turns to me. I just shake my head and turn up the TV. The game's about to start. Plus, this conversation is gettin' a little too weird for my taste.

Mike eventually stops strokin' his beard, and I grab a burger. But I can't get her out of my head. *Damn it*. She's not supposed to be there. She left. I forgot...or at least, I tried to. That's how it's supposed to be. She's supposed to be forgotten.

Chapter Eleven

Past (4 Years Earlier)

Rem

"I'll have a bacon cheeseburger with fries," I say to Kristen.

"Oh, and can I have a beer with mine?" Jack blurts out.

Kristen just rolls her eyes and looks to Owen. "What can I get ya, Owen?"

I'll just have the same thing as Rem," Owen says. "And I'll take a beer." Owen looks over at Jack and just smiles. Jack looks back at him with a scowl.

"Now, you can have one," Kristen says, smilin' at Owen. And none of us miss the wink she gives him either.

Kristen turns then and heads back behind the bar.

"You got a ways until you're twenty-one, don't ya?" Owen asks Jack. "If I remember right, I believe you were *still in diapers by the time I started school."*

"Shit, you don't remember that," Jack cuts back.

"I remember you two babies cryin' in the principal's office that day Miss Evans caught ya cheatin'," Owen says.

"Oh, here we go," I say, sittin' back in my chair.

"Well," Jacks says, gaining momentum, "we wouldn't have been cheatin' if someone hadn't told us that it would be a good idea to write the times tables on our arms in permanent marker right before the test."

"Hey, I didn't tell ya to wear short sleeves," Owen says. "I was only tryin' to help ya."

"Yeah, help us wind up in Mr. Geriatric's office," Jack says. "It was May. It was hotter than shit that day. And we were supposed to wear long sleeves?"

"Here ya go, honey," Kristen says, slidin' a beer across the table to Owen.

"Thanks, sweet cheeks," Owen says, smilin' back at her.

Jack cringes at Owen and Kristen's exchange, as Kristen turns and walks off.

"Hey, where's mine?" Jack hollers to her back.

"It's sittin' in the cooler," she says, not even botherin' to turn around. "And it'll keep on sittin' in there for a few more years."

Jack looks back at us and just sighs.

"Now, you see that, dunderheads." Owen points the neck of his bottle in the direction of Kristen. "There are some things in this world you just don't take for granted, and that," he says, pausin' to lock eyes with Kristen across the bar. He smiles at her. She smiles back. "That is one of them."

Owen kicks the leg of Jack's chair and takes a swig of his beer.

"Who? Kris?" Jack asks. He's half scowlin', half grinnin'.

Owen refuses to say anything in response, so Jack turns

to me instead. I just shrug. Owen doesn't usually say things like that. Of course, Owen is Owen. I stopped questionin' him a long time ago.

"Geezer wisdom," Jack pipes up, a big grin takin' over his face all of a sudden. "That's what Owen's got."

I look at Owen and laugh. "Must be," I agree.

"Ya old geezer," Jack says, through a laugh.

"Hey, call it whatever you want," Owen says. "I still get to drink my beer out in public, while you two dunderheads gotta sit here with your sippy cups of Coke." He takes another swig and shakes his head. He's got this fake, sympathetic look on his face now.

I can tell Jack doesn't know what to say to that. Hell, I don't have a comeback either. So, we all just sit there starin' at each other, until Jack finally starts laughin', and then I join in, and finally, Owen does too.

"What are you guys all laughin' about?" Kristen asks. She stops at our table and sets down three plates of burgers and fries.

"Oh, nothin'," Jack says. "We're just learnin' what fun-filled life we got waitin' for us at twenty-one. In fact, in the time it took Owen to finish his beer, I've already looked into a nice retirement home for myself."

"What?" Kristen gives Jack a puzzled look.

"Oh, Jack's just got his panties in a bunch; that's all," Owen says.

"What's new?" Kristen asks, smilin' at Jack.

Jack just rolls his eyes, while I take a big bite of my burger and watch as Kristen steals a fry from Owen's plate and pops it into her mouth.

"Now, you boys stay out of trouble tonight," she says, smilin' at me this time. "Or at least, tell me, so I can come too."

"Of course," Owen says, givin' Kristen a wink.

With that, Kristen turns on her heels and heads back to the bar. And not even a second later, Owen kicks Jack's chair again.

"What the hell?" Jack barks.

"Remember what I said," Owen warns.

"Yeah, whatever, geezer," Jack says, smilin' wide, despite his mouth full of food.

Chapter Twelve

Present

I'm in Sunny Square. The vendors are out. There are people all around me. Mike is here. He's wearin' his old Cardinals cap and laughin' over at Joe's Kettle Korn. But something is off; something's not right.

I allow my eyes to quickly sweep the street. Jack is here, too. He's leanin' up against the theater's brick side talkin' to Kristen. She's got a smile on her face. Jack does, too. The sun is out, but the air feels thick. I briefly close my eyes and try to breathe it in.

"How much for the quilt?"

I open my eyes and look up. Some older guy I don't recognize—probably because he's from out of town—is starin' at me. He's hovering over a faded blue and yellow quilt. It's my quilt. Ashley found it at an antique store one hot day in July. She said I had to have it. "It will make your living room look more like a home." I play her words back in my head.

The quilt is lyin' across the couch that Ashley and I would spend our lazy afternoons on, watchin' reruns of Seinfeld and old Humphrey Bogart movies.

"How much?" the old man asks. His voice is getting impatient.

"Uh, it's not for sale."

He gives me a strange look. "Then why's it out here?"

I don't answer him. I don't know what to say. I don't know why it's out here. He frowns at me and then marches off with an older, gray-haired woman, who, I assume is his wife.

My eye catches on an old hockey stick next. It's mine. I used my lawn-cutting money to buy it from a sporting goods store when I was twelve. I was going through a hockey phase. It lasted a couple months. It's a left-handed stick. I'm right-handed. I didn't know any different back then. But why is it out here? Why is all my stuff out here?

"How much for this lamp?"

I turn around. A brunette, who's maybe in her twenties, is starin' back at me, holdin' up a big, green lamp.

"Ten dollars," I say. Ashley hated that lamp.

The girl gives me a ten-dollar bill and walks away with the green lamp.

"How much for this?"

Before I can even look up, I recognize the voice. "Ashley."

She's holdin' up the bamboo plant—her love plant.

I'm nearly breathless just lookin' at her.

"Can we talk?" I ask.

"I can't." Her smile fades and is quickly replaced by a thick coat of sympathy. "I'm with my husband."

"You're married?" My heart sinks to the deepest crevasse of my chest.

She nods and sets the plant back down.

"Hey, buddy, Kristen said Caleb is havin' some people over later." Jack is, all of a sudden, in front of me. I look at him and then back to Ashley, but she's gone.

"Not now," I tell Jack.

I scan the crowd of men and women and kids and dogs on leashes, turnin' on my heels as I do it, and before I get all the way around, Ashley is back.

"Come on," she says. "Walk with me."

She takes off toward the river. I'm so nervous or dumbfounded, it takes me several seconds before I pick up my feet and follow after her.

"You're married?" I ask her again, once I've caught up to her. The scent of her perfume brings my senses to life and forces me to remember how much I've missed her.

"Yes, just married," she says. She holds out the ring. But she might as well have held out a knife.

"Well, he's a lucky guy." I'm surprised at how calmly I say the words. I'm surprised at how calm I am.

I follow her to the bench that overlooks the river. The water is dark and murky and eerie. I've never seen it like this.

She sits down, and I do, too. She's wearin' a long, white gown. It's slit up the side, and a corner is blowin' up in the breeze, exposin' the tanned skin of her thigh.

"We sat here once," I say to her, takin' a breath. The air's no longer thick. "Do you remember? It was our first date."

She smiles. "Of course I remember."

I feel my lips turn up at that. Something about her thinkin' about a memory that only we share makes me happy again...for a moment.

"Why does it have to hurt so much?" I ask.

Her smile fades a little. "It's not supposed to be painless, Rem. It's supposed to be worth it."

I take in her words. She said that same phrase once when we were together. But she had said it with a smile. It was after I had sat through an entire special viewing of *Titanic*—the one with Leonardo DiCaprio drawin' pictures and pretendin' to fly on a boat for almost four hours. This time, however, her words strike me in a whole different way. And at the same time, I notice the river is clear now. It's clear like creek water. I can see straight to the bottom. And I definitely know I've never seen it this way, but I quickly dismiss it.

"Ashley, I'm sorry. There's so much I would take back."

Her lips don't move. She just looks up at me with a sad expression glazin' her face. I look into her eyes for several seconds, and then I look away. The story of our time together is written on the green in her eyes, and I don't want to read it. I look down at the grassy ground by my feet instead, as the sound of a freight train roars behind us. "I loved you so much," I go on. "I loved you so much more than I showed you. I'm so sorry." I stop to take a breath, but I still don't look up. "Ashley, I love you. I'll always love you."

It's so quiet. Everything's so quiet. I no longer hear the voices from Sunny Square in the background. The hum from the train that just went by has disappeared. And the air is like mud again.

I try to take another breath, and I look up, and Ashley's gone. Immediately, it feels as if a knife jabs straight into my heart.

"She didn't hear any of it," I whisper, as it sinks in.

I sit back against the iron bench. There's an ache so strong in my throat that I can hardly get a breath, or even swallow; I'm devastated. I don't question why she left or if she were ever really there at all. My mind is just so consumed with the fact that she didn't hear anything that I needed her to hear. She didn't hear any of it—not even a word.

I close my eyes. Liquid forms behind my eyelids, though for some reason or another, I can't feel it; I just sense it. And when I open my eyes, there's another train. It sounds its whistle so loudly that it startles me. And the whistle doesn't stop either. It's just one continuous, high-pitched noise. And it sounds as if it's getting closer. I stand up and turn toward the sound. And immediately, I notice the train is off its tracks. It's comin' straight for me. I try to move, but I can't. My feet are cemented to the ground. So instead, I close my eyes and prepare for impact.

My eyes snap open.

I'm in my bed. My alarm is blarin' from the cardboard box I use as a night table. I swipe at it, and the room goes silent.

I turn on my back and look up at the ceiling. I'm breathing heavily. *It was just a dream.*

"It was just a dream," I whisper to myself.

I rub my eyes with the palms of my hands and then slide my fingers through my hair. I feel as if there's a thirty-pound weight sittin' on my chest.

"Ashley," I whisper, suddenly recallin' the rest of the dream.

I jump up and run to my laptop. It's at my kitchen table where I left it the night before. I log onto Jack's Facebook and type *Ashley Westcott* into the search box. We're not Facebook friends. We haven't been since the day she left.

I click on her *About* section and quickly scroll down through her place of work and where she lives. It doesn't say she's married. I go back to her timeline. Workin' quickly, I scroll past photos of her and her friends, smilin' and havin' fun; shots of a little brown and white beagle; pictures of a sunset over a lake. But there's no wedding photos.

She's not married. I breathe a sigh of relief.

This is crazy. Of course she's not married. I just saw her. She would have told me if she were married. *Right?* Hell, maybe not; I don't know. Anyway, I would have seen the ring.

I close the laptop and shut my eyes. I try to hear her laughter. I try to imagine it just as it is. I try really hard. And then, just like that, I can hear it. I can hear the soft hitch in her voice—its low and high pitches, the ones that make it distinctly hers. It's her laugh...exactly. My heart swells.

It's funny how you can remember somethin' like someone's laugh, how you can just close your eyes and think real hard and just recall it. It's the gift—and the curse—of memory, I guess. It's yours to keep, whether you like it or not.

I take a breath and listen to it—to her—as if she's right next to me.

And then, it's as if from somewhere deep inside my

soul, a soft, clear voice rises up and echoes the words of my heart: *I wish. I wish she were right next to me.*

Chapter Thirteen

Past (2 Years Earlier)

Rem

*"**M**iss Westcott, has anyone ever told you that you have the prettiest eyes?"*

It's a lazy Saturday. Those still exist in this small town. We're along the river downtown, takin' in the way the world has just, all of a sudden, turned orange and red—just like it does every fall. Her back's against this old maple tree, and it's just the two of us against the world.

She smiles and bows her head before findin' my eyes again. I already figured someone had to have told her that by now.

"Well, then, has anyone ever told you that your eyes look oddly similar to mine?"

She laughs to herself as her stare turns down again. "No," she says, lookin' back up at me. "No one's ever told me that my eyes look oddly similar to Remington Jude's eyes."

"They do," I assure her. "I think they're the same color...almost."

"Almost?" she asks.

"Yeah," I say, "yours have this little touch of dark to them, like the sky does on one of those days. You know, the kind of day when you don't know if it's about to open up and throw down a funnel of wind or buckets of water?"

She just looks up at me. She's biting her bottom lip. It distracts me so much that I can't take my eyes off her mouth, and soon enough, my lips are touchin' hers.

The kiss is momentary, but the moment seems as if it hangs in the air—suspended like a bird in the wind. And in that moment, my heart is full, and my life is hers. I know it. She knows it. We both know, without sayin' a word, that no matter what happens between the two of us, I will always belong to this girl.

"Ashley?"

"Mm-hmm?"

"I really like you," I say, softly restin' my forehead onto hers. My heart is beatin' so hard in my chest that I feel as if I should be able to literally hear its thumps.

I kiss her sunburned lips again, and then I softly kiss her neck and then her suntanned collarbone. I couldn't possibly feel any more for this girl. I've already given her everything I have. And I should be scared as hell knowin' that, but I'm not—not even one bit.

"How did you know my name?" she asks.

"What?"

"At the dance, you knew my name. We hadn't met."

I look down at the grass at our feet. "Oh, that."

She smiles. "Yeah, that."

"I asked," I say, shruggin' my shoulders. "Carol, at Sander's Market, knew. She must have seen your name on your debit card or somethin'."

"Aah," she says, slowly nodding.

"Yeah," I go on, "the first time I saw you, you were in the store, and you were wearin' this tee shirt that was tied in a knot at the bottom. And you had this lace..."

"Crocheted."

"What?"

"Crocheted. The skirt," she says.

"Yeah, I guess. You had this crocheted, long, black skirt on with flip flops. And your hair was down, and it was wavy. And I just... You looked up at me...and it was as if your eyes cut right through me. And I know this sounds crazy, but you literally took my breath away. I just had to know your name. So, as soon as you left, I asked Carol."

"You remember all that?" she asks.

"Of course. How could I forget? That image of you standin' there is tattooed on my brain. I don't think I could forget even if I wanted to. And I don't...want to."

Her smile grows as she leans into me. I put my arms around her and let my hands rest on the bare part of her back. She's wearin' one of those cut-off tee shirts. I savor the way her soft skin feels against my fingertips.

"Wait," I say, pullin' away from her a little. "How do you remember what you were wearin' when I first saw you?"

She bows her head before lookin' into my eyes. "It was the first time I saw you, too. I was wearing a white top and the skirt. You were wearing a gray, Cardinals tee shirt and dark jeans. I was buying orange juice. You were holding a carton of milk. And you stopped. You literally stopped and looked up at me. And I smiled at you. And you didn't smile back."

I laugh once. "What?"

"You didn't smile back," she repeats.

"No, that's not me. I would have smiled at you."

"You didn't."

"That's crazy talk," I say.

"I'm serious. You just looked at me for a couple seconds, and then you looked down at your milk, as if you were reading its ingredients or something."

I swipe my hand across my eyes and then let my fist fall to my heart. *"The ingredients? Wow! And you still let me dance with you later?"*

She laughs. *"You're lucky that it was only my first week here, and by that time, I was beginning to think that was the customary greeting. It's like no one knew whether they should befriend me or run from me."*

I pull her even closer and press my lips to her neck. *"No, sweetheart, we're just shy around beautiful creatures, that's all."*

I can feel her laugh, but I just keep kissin' her neck.

"Did I stick out?"

"What?" I ask.

"When I first got here, did I look different or something?"

"Sweetie," I say, lookin' into her eyes this time, *"everybody who isn't from here sticks out."*

She drops her stare, and her voice hitches a little.

"No, but seriously," I say, regaining her attention. *"You'd probably stick out anywhere."*

"What does that mean?" She looks at me as if she's almost hesitant to ask.

"It means that no matter where you are or what you're wearin' or who you're with, people would notice you. You've got like this...bubble around you."

"What?"

"Yeah," I say, *"I can't explain it. It's just, when you smile at me, it's like I think if I can just get nearer to you—if I could just get inside that bubble—then everything in the world would be right. And I can't be the only one that thinks that."*

"Rem," she scolds with a smile, *"you're probably the only person in this world that thinks I live in a bubble."*

"No," I say, shakin' my head. "I can't be. But if you are right by some messed-up, out-of-kilter way of thinkin', then I'm the luckiest man in the world because I see a treasure that no one else can see."

She leans into me and sweetly kisses my cheek.

"Wait," I say, "you remember the first time you saw me?"

She looks into my eyes. "Of course."

I just smile, and I'm still smilin' several seconds later.

"Rem," she whispers, standin' on tiptoe and restin' her lips near my ear. At the same time, a shiver runs up my spine. "You wanna know why?"

"Yeah," I barely get out.

"You took my breath away, too."

I feel my smile growin'.

"And you know what else?" she whispers, kissin' my cheek and then lookin' into my eyes.

"Yeah?"

"I really like you, too."

Chapter Fourteen

Present

I'm in the grocery store, pickin' up some bread and some beer—two of my staples. I'm starin' at a small section of the bread aisle. I'm tryin' to eat healthier. *Tryin'* is the key word. I try to remember the bread Ashley always used to get. She was probably one of the healthiest people I knew—though I know that's not sayin' much, if you consider my circle of friends. But Ashley would eat things that just sounded strange, like sushi and quinoa and stuff like that, which I eventually just equated to healthy. They didn't sell that stuff anywhere around here, so we'd have to go to the city to get it. It didn't taste like much to me, and I always had to have a bowl of cereal afterward because I was still hungry. But I ate it because she said it was "healthy," and mostly, because it made her smile.

My eyes scan the labels: white, wheat, oat, potato. *Potato?* What? Hell, they're makin' bread out of everything these days.

"I heard she left town because he caught her cheatin' on him."

A girl's voice permeates through the wall behind the bread. It sounds as if she's in the next aisle. And it doesn't sound as if she's tryin' to keep whatever she's talkin' about a secret.

"I heard it was because he cheated on her," I hear another girl say.

I don't recognize the voices or know who they're talkin' about, and I don't really care either. They're probably high schoolers, talkin' about whatever high school girls talk about these days, which is probably not that much different from what high schoolers talked about ten, twenty, fifty years ago.

"If I were Ashley, I would have left too, then."

Immediately, I stop carin' about the bread and go completely still. Just like that, at her name, I suddenly care about what the high school girls on the other side of the bread aisle are sayin'.

"But if you ask me," the same voice says, "I don't think he could have cheated on her. They were such a cute couple."

"Maybe she just went crazy," the other says. "I mean, beautiful people do crazy things sometimes, right? The stars are always doin' crazy stuff. And she was from where? Iowa?"

"Nebraska," the higher-pitched voice corrects.

"Same difference," the other says. "All I know is that she wasn't from here."

"But yeah," the one goes on. "Maybe you're right. Maybe she just went crazy in this little town."

"Hey, you know, I did hear Rem was with Kristen Sawyer now."

"Hall's Kristen?" the one asks.

"Yep," the other confirms.

Then I hear feet shufflin' along the vinyl, and I quickly grab a loaf of bread, not carin' which one is which anymore.

I don't know what to think about the conversation. How do two high schoolers know anything about me and Ashley? And why do they care? Why does anyone care?

I tuck the bread under my arm and head straight for the register, forgetting the beer. I don't care what this whole, damn town thinks about what happened between me and Ashley. They don't need to know.

I get home and toss the bread and my keys onto the counter. Jack is sittin' on my couch, yellin' at the TV. I expected to see him in here. His truck's parked out front.

"Hey, have you heard I'm with Kristen?"

"What?" He mutes the TV and dramatically careens his neck around, as if he's just now noticed me.

"Evidently, I'm with Kristen now," I say again.

"What are you talkin' about?" He's wearin' this dumb, hurt look on his face.

"Rumor," I say. "It's just a rumor. Relax, buddy." I throw up my hands in surrender. *Yeah, Jack doesn't have a thing for Kristen, my ass.*

"Oh, yeah," he says, turnin' back around. Instantly, he seems disinterested. "I heard that one."

"What?"

"Yeah," he says, "whoever you heard that from, they need to check their supplier. That's old news. I heard about that almost a year ago."

"What? Why didn't you say anything?"

He shrugs. "I don't know. I knew it wasn't true. I just threw it on the pile."

I cock my head. "Pile?"

"Yeah, there's more where that came from."

Jack keeps his eyes on the TV. I just keep mine on Jack.

"Wait, what do you mean?" I ask.

He puts his hand to his mouth, as if he's recalling something, and then he looks back at me. "All right, so when you and Ashley were together, you had a secret love child, you ran away and got married...twice...and...you were secretly a millionaire." He looks off to the side, as if he's thinkin' again. "Wait, the millionaire thing was a rumor I made up about myself. Nobody thought you were a millionaire."

"Oh," I say, sarcastically. "That's a relief."

He unmutes the television, and his eyes go back to followin' the ball on a rerun of an old Bulls game.

"They say she went crazy," I say.

"Who?"

"Ashley."

He glances at me for a half-second and then looks back at the TV. "Yeah, well, maybe she did. That would explain why she left so fast." He pauses and picks up a bottle from the floor. "But she ain't the first one to leave this place. And she won't be the last, either." He takes a swig from the bottle and sets it back down. "But, yeah, maybe she did go crazy."

My eyes leave Jack for the television, as I suck in a deep breath and then slowly force it right back out.

Or maybe she didn't.

Chapter Fifteen

Past (1.5 Years Earlier)

Rem

*"**O**kay, so the holler's the best place to find 'em," I say, stoppin' the truck near the silage pit.*

"Holler?"

"Uh, yeah." I point with my eyes straight ahead.

"What is a holler?"

"You're in it, sweetheart."

"Oh." She looks around, like she's examinin' the place. "Well, I don't think we have anything called a holler in West Omaha."

I just stare at her with what I'm sure is a pretty damned amused look on my face. "Girl, you'd think you grew up in New York City. I know you've got corn fields all around Omaha. Surely, you've got somethin' you call a holler."

She sucks in a quick breath through her teeth and just

shakes her head. "I don't think so."

"Really?"

"I mean, yeah, we might have a lot of corn fields," she says, "but just because you've got girls hangin' all over you, it doesn't make you an expert in them, now does it?"

"Well..." I cock my head to the side. She just laughs. "All right. All right. You got me," I concede.

"But seriously," she goes on, "people might think Omaha's not such a big place in the whole scheme of things and that corn is all we know, but to be honest, I've never even been in a corn field. And I sure don't know what a holler is."

I just look over at her and smile. "Well, okay, city girl, get your cute butt out of this truck because I'm about to give you a lesson in country."

She giggles and slides off the seat. I get out too and meet her at the front of the truck.

"Okay," I say, pointin' straight ahead. "This here is the holler. There's not much here anymore. My grandpa used to have hogs down here. But now, it's pretty much just some old outbuildings and a lot of trees—good for findin' mushrooms."

"But what's it mean? Holler?" She says the word again, rollin' it off her tongue as if it's a foreign language. Actually, I've never heard holler *sound so sexy. And I'm tryin' to push that thought to the back of my mind when I notice her starin' up at me.*

"Oh," I start. "You know what?" I cover my mouth partially with my hand. "Well, it's supposed to mean a valley, I think." I look around. "But you know what? We're not really in a valley, are we?"

She looks around, too, and just smiles. "I don't think we are."

I'm earnestly stumped. "My grandpa always called this place the holler. My dad did, too. But in all that time, I never asked why."

Her soft laughter distracts me for a second. "How are you supposed to teach me all this stuff if you don't even know why it is?"

"Oh, sweetheart," I say, givin' her a confident grin. "That's the beauty of livin' out here. You'll learn pretty quickly that things—and words—just get passed down. Around here, not many people question things. Now, as a kid, you might try to ask why. *But not many people will give you a straight answer. And I don't know if that's just because they never knew the answer to begin with or if they just don't want to tell ya or if they just plain forgot."*

A smile stretches across her pretty face. "I don't know if I should laugh or cry at that."

"As I've said, we're a simple people, Miss Westcott."

Her voice starts to hitch again. I listen to the way it hangs in the air, and at the same time, I try to hold onto every piece of it.

"Okay," I say, once her sweet voice starts to fade, "so we're lookin' for the ones that look like little Christmas trees."

"Christmas trees," she repeats. "Got it."

We shuffle our feet over the soggy leaves that layered the ground all winter. The sun is high and peekin' through the trees now, and there's a fresh smell of spring in the air.

"Now, this is an oak tree." I stop and touch my hand to a tall, thick trunk. "If you see one of these, it'd be a good idea to look around it. Oaks like sun. So do morels."

"Oak. Sun. Mushrooms. Got it." She shuffles around the back of the tree. I just watch her. I know she's excited. She gets this look when she's excited. It's as if she's tryin' her damnedest not to smile, but she's smilin' anyway. And her eyes get this spark to them, like she's seein' everything for the very first time.

"Rem!"

I'm jolted out of my train of thought as I round the backside of the tree to find her. "You find one?"

"No, but I did find a cool rock."

"A rock?"

"Look." She holds it out to me. "It's a perfect heart."
She turns it over in her hand. There's that happy glint in her
eyes.

"You sure you didn't just chisel that right now?" I ask,
examinin' the rock.

"Well, I suppose I haven't told you about my excellent
chiseling skills yet." She laughs and catches my gaze. We
grow quiet then, and all I want to do is kiss her. I move
closer to her, but before I get to her lips, I notice her eye
catch on something.

"Wait, is that one?"

I look to where she's pointin'. "Well, I'll be. I think you
just found your first morel, Miss Westcott."

She smiles wide, and then shortly after, I notice her grin
slowly startin' to fade. "Now, what do I do?"

I try to swallow down the laugh formin' in my chest and
movin' up my throat. "You pick it."

She looks at the mushroom and then back at me and
then at the mushroom again. You would have thought I had
just told her to pick up a copperhead or somethin'. But
eventually, she moves closer to the mushroom, bends down
low to the ground and slowly forces her hand toward the
morel.

"Is it bad that I'm afraid to touch it? It looks kind
of...squishy...and weird."

I can't help but laugh at that. "It is *squishy and weird!*
But it tastes good, and it's not gonna bite ya." I rock back on
my heels. "Though, I did have one sting me once."

She pulls her hand back faster than a cat jumpin' out of
a tub of cold water.

"I'm only kiddin'," I say.

"Rem!" She smacks my pant leg and lets out a puff of
air.

"I'm sorry. I'll stop," I promise.

She playfully rolls her eyes at me, and then in one swift motion, plucks the mushroom from the ground.

And as she holds it out to me, I settle in her arresting stare. She looks so proud...and so happy. And all that's runnin' through my mind is: I love this girl, I love this girl, I love this girl. I lean into her and kiss those happy lips of hers, and when our kiss breaks, I squeeze her against my chest and give her a peck on her head.

"Okay," I say, breathin' in the sweet scent of her hair, "so let's find a handful more, and then we'll go make the best sandwich you've ever tasted."

"You mind if we fry 'em up at my parents'?"

"Your parents'?"

"Yeah, it's closer. Plus, I'm almost positive that I don't have eggs...or flour...or a fryin' pan."

She laughs, and it makes me laugh, too. I could have gone and bought all that stuff before today, but I think there's a big part of me that wants my parents to meet Ashley. I think it's a I-just-want-to-show-her-off-to-the-world kind of thing.

"But I'm not really dressed for meeting the parents." I watch her look down at her blue jeans and pink tennis shoes.

"Horse shit," I say. "You look beautiful."

Her eyes instantly rush to mine. She's got this big, surprised look on her face, like she's never heard anyone say horse shit *or call her* beautiful *before—and I know that last one ain't true.*

"Okay, then," she concedes, breathing out a smile.

"You're not nervous, are you?"

She presses her lips together and closes her eyes. "Maybe a little."

"Of my parents?"

"I don't know. Yeah?"

*"You don't have to be nervous of them. They'll love
you. And if it makes you feel any better, my mom's a teacher.
And she's even got a soft spot for the kid that tries to eat
rocks on the playground every recess."*

"Am I like the kid that eats rocks?"

"Not quite," I say, with a straight face.

She puts a little pout on.

"I'm kiddin', baby."

"Baby?"

*I alternate my eyes between her and the road. I took a
risk with the "baby" thing. Maybe she doesn't like it.
Seconds draw on. She's really makin' me sweat here. And
just when I'm about to take it back, her questioning stare
gives way to a smile, and I let go of a thankful breath.*

*I watch her over there in the passenger's seat then, as
she watches me. There's somethin' in the way she's lookin'
at me that's drivin' me wild. Damn, this girl's really got a
hold on me! I'd pull this truck over right now if it weren't
daylight...and I had a place other than the ditch to pull it
into... Shit! What the hell!*

*I bring the truck to a quick stop—right in the middle of
the road. And just like that, her pretty stare turns
challengin'. It's as if we were both thinkin' the same thing.*

*And then without another thought or even so much as a
word between us, I slide closer to her. She meets me
halfway, and instantly, our lips collide. And before I know it,
one hand's pressin' against the small of her back and one's
tangled in her hair. And I don't miss the fact that she's
twistin' the hem of my tee shirt into one of her hands and
pullin' on my neck with the other.*

*I press my mouth hard against hers. She hungrily moves
her lips along mine, and with that, our kiss deepens. I'm
used to slow and gentle kisses with this girl. But this one is
all fire and passion and heat, and I'm lovin' every second of
it, until somethin' stops us right in our tracks.*

It's almost as if a damn wreckin' ball just comes and

plows right through the cab. A loud, dull horn startles us apart. Our eyes quickly move toward the sound only to find a jacked-up pickup truck that I don't recognize sittin' right behind us.

"Damn it," I breathe out. I gently press my forehead against hers, and I don't know how, but a smile finds its way to my face.

She lowers her eyes and starts to laugh.

Another honk.

"Damn it to hell," I say again, shaking my head. If the road were wide enough, I'd just wave him on.

"Can we pick this up later?" I ask her, her hair still wrapped around my fingers.

Her eyes meet mine, and she just smiles and then nods.

"Okay," I say, almost as if I'm givin' myself a pep talk—tellin' myself that I can, in fact, leave this girl and get my ass back behind that wheel, even though I'm already kickin' myself for even thinkin' about it.

"Okay," I say again, right before I reluctantly climb back into the driver's seat and put her into gear. And just like that, we're moseyin' down that gravel road again. It seems to pacify the guy behind us. But I'm not too worried about him. In fact, I think I'd still be silently cursin' his name—whoever he is—if it weren't for her. I look over at Ashley. She's runnin' her fingers through her hair and pressin' her lips together when she catches my gaze and smiles.

Damn it, I love her...and her soft lips and her smooth skin...and her long, tangled hair.

"Well, here we are," I say, pullin' off the county road and into my parents' drive.

"Already?"

"Hey," I say, gainin' her attention, "they'll love you."

She takes a big breath and then lets go of a half-grin, as we make our way down the long driveway.

About a minute later, we're both gettin' out of my truck and headin' inside. I call for Mom and Dad once we're in the house, but no one answers.

"Well, they're here," I say. "I just don't know where. They'll turn up. For now, let's get these mushrooms goin'.

We slice, wash and bread the morels, then stick them into a fryin' pan and fry them for a few minutes.

"Okay," I say, placin' a few of the fried slices onto a piece of white bread and foldin' the bread over. "Your first fried morel sandwich."

"Wait, you don't put anything on it?"

I shake my head. "Nope. Plain is best."

She smiles and just nods. "Plain is best," she repeats. Then she takes the sandwich, looks up at me, looks back at the sandwich and then takes a bite.

I watch her chew for a couple seconds. I don't know why, but I'm nervous all of a sudden. I have no idea why I want her to like this stupid sandwich so much.

She chews some more, then closes her eyes and swallows. And when she opens her eyes again and gazes into mine, I just can't take it anymore.

"Well, tell me, woman! Was that not the best sandwich you've ever tasted?"

She laughs and then, at last, nods her head. "You wanna know the truth?"

"Yes, the truth," I demand, barely able to control myself.

"That was the best sandwich I've ever tasted."

"Remington," I hear my mom call from the basement steps.

Ashley looks at me. She's got flour on her nose. I kiss the place where the flour is and then brush the rest of the white stuff away with the pad of my thumb.

"Oh, hi." My mom stops at the top of the basement

steps when she sees both of us.

"Hi," Ashley says, immediately holdin' out her hand.

Mom looks at her hand for a second. "Oh, sweetie, around here, we do hugs." She encloses Ashley in her arms. "And you must be the infamous Ashley," she states, as she pulls away.

Ashley looks back at me. She's got a little smile playin' on her face, like she doesn't quite know what to say about that, but she's not altogether mad about it, either.

"Oh, come on, I don't talk about her that much...do I?"

Mom rolls her eyes. Ashley keeps her pretty, little stare on me.

"Okay, fine, maybe I talk about you a little," I say to her, pinchin' my thumb and forefinger together.

"Cindy, where in tarnation did I put that drill?"

My dad barrels up the stairs, and within only a couple seconds, he's in the kitchen and starin' at us like we're two aliens invading his kitchen or somethin'.

"Oh," he says, "I didn't know we had company. I would have put on my good hat."

I gawk at him with what I'm sure is a puzzled look plastered to my face. "Dad, what in the hell is your good hat?"

"You know, it's that Cardinals one you got me. I save that one for company," he says, proudly sittin' back on his heels.

"Then, why have I never seen you wear it?"

"I don't know. Because you're not company."

"What about Jack and Mike?" I ask.

"Ha," he says. "You mean those other two kids I oddly don't remember bringin' home from the hospital—the ones that raid my refrigerator every Saturday and eat all my cheese dip?"

I just lower my head and laugh to myself. "Dad," I say, once I look up again. "This is Ashley."

"Hi, Mr. Jude," Ashley says, holdin' out her hand.

My dad takes her hand and shakes it. "It's Ken. Mr. Jude's only for Jack and Mike." He winks at Ashley, and Ashley just smiles.

"Were you guys makin' somethin'?" my mom asks.

"We just fried up some morels," I say.

"Oh, if there's any left, save me some," Dad interjects. "I've gotta find that dag nabbit drill."

And with that, he wanders off.

"Well, it was nice to meet you, Ashley," my mom says. "I'd stay and talk longer, but I've got the hose runnin' out back, and I've got to get my husband's drill." She covers her mouth and whispers the next part: "I hide it because he's always losin' it. That way, I know where it is when I need it."

Ashley gives my mom a big grin. "No, it's fine," she says, politely. "It was nice to meet you."

"We'll talk soon," my mom assures her, givin' her another hug. Then, she takes a couple steps and calls out to my dad: "I found it, honey." And a wink later, she's gone.

And with that, it's just Ashley and me alone in the kitchen again, and I can't help but pull her close to me.

"See, I told you they'd love you."

She squishes up her nose. "You think?"

"I know," I say, kissin' her squished-up nose.

Then I pull her into a hug and press her head to my chest. They really did love her. I could see it written all over their faces. And that makes me feel good.

"I want to meet your family," I whisper near her ear.

She pulls away from me. "You want to meet my family?"

"Yeah," I say. "And I want to see where you grew up."

"Really?"

"Yeah," I assure her.

It's as if she thinks about it for a second before she smiles and then finally nods. "Okay," she whispers.

"Yeah?" I ask.

"Yeah," she confirms, a big grin stretchin' across her pretty face.

Chapter Sixteen

Present

Rem

"Ashley."

She looks up at me, as if she's startled to see me.
"Rem. ...Hi."

"Hhh-i," I say. It's hard to imagine stumblin' over just one, two-lettered word, but I think I managed to do just that.

It's like the airport all over again, but at the same time, I think I was less surprised to see her there than here—at Hall's...in Ava.

"Well, what brings you back into town?" I ask.

The little smile she had quickly falls away. "I...um...just needed to come back, you know, for a moment. I needed to say some things to..."

I look down and nod my head. "I got it," I say, stopping her. I hear what she's not sayin'. I know why she's here. And I also know she didn't come here to talk to me.

When I look back up at her, I notice the soft smile has returned to her face. "So, it's good to be back," she says.

"Uh, yeah, I'm sure it is."

"I see we haven't stopped making rumors," she nearly whispers, glancin' across the bar.

I look over my shoulder and make eye contact with a couple I know from high school sittin' at a table across the room. Their stares immediately deflect to the floor when our eyes meet. I try not to laugh when I turn back to Ashley. "You have no idea."

She bows her head and grins. "Well, it's nice to see some things haven't changed."

"Yeah," I mumble.

Then that clock on the wall ticks out a few more loud seconds as neither one of us says anything.

"How's work?" she asks, finally breaking the quiet.

"It's great," I say, flatly. "Same old, same old."

Her lips turn down a little, and I know I'm not playin' nice. And it's in that moment that I realize I just have no idea how I'm supposed to act around her anymore.

I habitually refit my cap over my head and lean up against the bar. "How's the writing comin'?" I ask, tryin' to put more effort into the conversation.

All of a sudden, her expression is happy again. "It's going well. The book's almost done. There's a part of me that just can't wait for it all to be finished, but then, there's another part of me that is absolutely terrified. I'm literally terrified knowing that once it's published, actual, real people will be able to read it."

"Actual, real people," I confirm, smilin'.

She laughs and gives me this look she used to give me that I always thought meant she wanted to kiss me. And if I didn't know any better, I'd think that same thing today.

"How long are you in town?" I ask.

"I...um... I'm on my way out now, actually. I just stopped by to grab a tea for the road."

I nod, lettin' her statement sink in. I knew she wasn't here to stay or anything, but hearin' she's got one foot out the door already kind of stabs at my heart a little. And I know it shouldn't. Damn it, I know it shouldn't. She's not mine anymore. Hell, I don't even know if she were ever really mine. But damn it, I'm hers. As stupid and as impossible as that might sound, I'm hers. I know it. I know it deep in my soul. I'll never love another girl like I loved Ashley Westcott. I wonder if she knows that.

"You wanna know something?" she asks, breakin' me out of my thoughts. I can tell she's tryin' to cheer me up now. She might not know what I'm thinkin' exactly, but I'm certain she can read my face. And I'm certain it's not the happiest face I've ever put on. All the same, I look up at her a little surprised. I know I don't deserve her bein' nice to me.

"Sure," I say, agreein' to play along.

"I tried to make a mushroom sandwich."

"Yeah?" I ask.

"Well, I tried. I can't really make them like you can."

"Horse shit!" I blurt out. I say it a little too loud, and all eyes in the bar stop to look at me. Even Ashley looks at me, startled, right before she starts to laugh.

I watch her lips turn up as she tilts her face away from me. And then when she squares up to me again, I follow her hand as she tucks a strand of her long, blond hair behind her ear. And then she gives me that look—that look that makes me wish with everything I am that everything between us had turned out differently. And then I get a wild hair. It's a crazy idea. And it's probably stupid. But I can't help but be stupid sometimes. I think it's in my nature.

"Come on," I say, standin' up straight again.

"What?"

"I'll teach you again."

She gives me this look like I've just gone and lost my mind. "Where?"

"Here," I say.

"You can't teach me here." She shakes her head, almost as if she's shakin' off even the thought of it.

"Sure I can. Hold on. I've got some in my truck. I'll go get 'em."

"Of course," she says, her voice startin' to hitch. "Of course you've got mushrooms in your truck."

"What's the Boy Scout motto?" I ask, makin' my way across the bar.

"I don't know," she says, through quiet laughter.

"Always be prepared."

"But you were never a Boy Scout."

"Well, yeah, not a real one, technically, but that's only because everyone around here is just born a Boy Scout. We never really think to give it a title."

I leave her smilin' at the bar, as I push through the screen door and head for my truck. For the first time in a long time, I notice I have a little skip to my step.

I grab the mushrooms and fly back through the bar's back door not even a minute later and head for the kitchen.

"Rem, what are you doin'?" Kristen asks.

"Fryin' up some morels."

"What?"

"It's fine, Kristen," I say, assurin' her. "We'll be fast."

"You know, this is like 110 different health code violations," Kristen says, her hands on her hips.

"I won't tell," I promise.

She just rolls her eyes and heads back into the area where they keep all the tables and most of the people, while I set the morels next to the fryer and look back.

Ashley's at the door to the kitchen. "Come on," I say, wavin' her in. "It's okay."

It looks as if she contemplates it for a second before glancin' over at Kristen.

"Might as well," Kristen says, shruggin' her shoulders. "I've never won against a Jude. I don't even try to fight it anymore."

Ashley smiles and then looks back at me, and before I know it, she's plantin' her feet right next to mine.

"That's my girl," I say.

She gives me a half-scoldin' look before her lips turn up at their corners. *I'll take that.*

"Okay, so let's get some breading materials together," I say, lookin' for the flour.

"Ohhh..." The word that escapes her mouth sounds somewhat defeated.

I stop and look at her. She's got this half-smile, half-revelation thing goin' on. "Let me guess. You didn't bread 'em?" I ask.

She closes her eyes and squishes up her little nose. I just throw my head back and laugh at the ceiling.

We make the sandwiches, but mostly, we laugh. It couldn't have been more than fifteen minutes, and there's flour everywhere. It's even on her forehead. And I can't help but love everything about this moment. I wish it didn't have to end. I already know I'm gonna miss it when it's gone.

I take a bite into the bread and the morels, and I look over at her. She's sittin' on the counter, swingin' her legs and chewin' away. I could stare at her all day, and I both hate and love that thought.

"Jeez, Rem!" Kristen steps inside the kitchen and throws her hands on her hips.

Her shrill voice startles the both of us. I stand up. Ashley jumps off the counter, and when her feet hit the grease-covered floor, she loses her balance. I notice she's fallin', so I drop my sandwich and slip my arm around her waist. And for a moment, she stops fallin' and looks into my eyes. And I see my Ashley. And I swear she sees me.

"Okay...well," Kristen stutters, soundin' now almost as if she's sorry for interruptin' somethin'. "Karen's comin' in for her shift soon. Just make it look half descent again."

I'd turn around, but I already know Kristen's gone. So instead, I make sure Ashley is steady, and then I back away a step.

She straightens her tee shirt and brushes back a few stray strands of her hair. "Thanks," she whispers.

I just nod. I can't seem to find any good words to say. She's starin' at me, and I'm starin' back at her. There's somethin' still between us. I can feel it. But after a moment, she looks away, clears her throat and grabs the bag of flour, solidifyin' the fact that the moment's gone. And I just stand there and sigh inwardly for what feels like an eternity, before reachin' for my sandwich on the floor.

We get everything put away and all the counters wiped down before I walk her out to her car.

"Hey," I say, "you'll send me a book when it's finished, right?"

She gives me that look that I never could quite figure out. I don't know if it's sympathy or sadness or somewhere in between. "Sure," she says, nodding.

Then, she turns and gets into her car.

"Hey," I say, regaining her attention.

I wait until I can see her face.

"If everything were different, would we be together?"

Little wrinkles form on her forehead. I can tell she's thinkin'. "Do you mean that if I lived in a fairy tale, and that if you lived in a fairy tale, and that if we both lived in that fairy tale together, would we be together?"

I slowly nod. "Yeah," I say. "Somethin' like that."

I notice her smile, right before she bobs her head. "Yeah," she says. "I think we might." She stops and takes a moment before sayin' her next words. "If there are happily ever afters in life, we just might have a chance, but..."

She doesn't finish her sentence, but it doesn't matter. I already know how it ends. I take a deep breath and bob my head, too, knowingly—knowing we will never get our happily ever after.

"Rem?"

"Yeah?"

She's pressin' her lips together and lookin' away, like she wants to say somethin'.

"Never mind," she says, shakin' it off.

"You sure?"

Say somethin', Ashley. Please say somethin'.

I know I can't change a damn thing between us, so I

don't know why I torture myself. But I just can't help but want her to believe in us—even if all the odds are against us, even if we screwed it all up, even if it's all just a lie.

"Yeah," she says, lookin' up at me with her pretty eyes. "It's nothing."

"Okay," I whisper, unwillingly.

She starts up her car, and I hand her her tea right before I lightly tap the hood and step back.

"Well, take care, Ash."

"You too, Rem."

And with that, she slowly pulls out of the gravel parking lot. I watch her car until it disappears about a half mile down the road. And then, she's gone—she's gone just as quickly as she had come. And I'm just left with a memory of a moment in an old bar's tiny kitchen—a sweet, perfect memory, forever frozen in time, where we were almost *us* again.

Chapter Seventeen

Past (1.5 Years Earlier)

Rem

"Hey, Mr. Katz." *I tip my cap to his stone. Then I turn to Owen's. "Hey, buddy," I say, noticin' somethin' hidden behind several blades of grass. It's another postcard. I reach down and pick it up.*

This time, the card reads Fiji.

I flip it over. As usual, there's nothin' on the back. It's blank, except for the four lines that mark where an address is supposed to go.

I turn the card back over. A photo of an island covered in palm trees and surrounded by blue-green water makes up the front of the card. I look deeper into the photo, tryin' to imagine bein' there. It looks so exotic, so different from what I'm used to. Even the colors don't seem like any I've ever seen in real life. Hell, the place might as well be on a different planet; I can't even imagine bein' somewhere like that.

I set the card back down against the gravestone and take my seat on my little stool.

"So, you might know this already. Or maybe you don't. I don't know what you can see up there." I take my cap off, run my hand through my hair and then go to habitually squeezin' the cap's bill until its sides are touching. "I met a girl," I blurt out.

I sit there quietly after I say it, imaginin' what Owen would say next.

"Man, I know what you're thinkin': Girls are trouble. Girls aren't worth it...*"*

I tug at my jeans and stretch the fabric back down to the bottom of my boots.

"I get it, and I hear ya, but this girl's different. I mean, she's beautiful. And she's, sure as hell, smarter than I am. That's gotta count for somethin'." I laugh and rest my cap on my bended knee. "And she's kind, like really kind—like kinder than I've ever seen anybody be around here. I mean, you can really tell she cares about people. You know how most people here are. They see somethin' every day, and it just becomes a part of life. No one ever thinks to change it up or anything. But she does. Hell, yesterday, she bought Crazy Kip a meal from Nancy's Diner, 'just because,' she said. And I know it sounds crazy, but she's got this story in her eyes, and I want to know it. I want to know everything about her." I look up at the dark-blue-and-white-painted sky and then level my gaze on the tree in front of us. "This girl," I say, shakin' my head. "She's just... She's city. And well, you know, I'm pretty country. But she can sit through rush hour and not be fazed by it. Yet, she can also sit on a porch swing and just watch the sun go down for hours. And oh, man, is she sexy! Jeez, I could go on about that for days." I stop to laugh. "But I won't torture you with that. And I guess what I'm tryin' to say is she's so much of everything at one

*time that she makes her own type of real...and beautiful." I
stop on that word, not even carin' that Owen would be
makin' fun of me right about now for even sayin' the word
beautiful.*

*"I just wasn't expectin' her, you know? I didn't see her
comin'. But, I guess, it doesn't really matter, does it? She's
here, and I'm here, and I'm glad that I'm here with her."*

*I mindlessly pick up a rock and trace its edges with the
tips of my fingers. "Plus, you can't give me too much shit. I
know all about your girlfriend. Maybe you could hide the
fact that you were in love in life, but you sure as hell aren't
very good at it now."*

*I smile and let the rock drop from my hands. "You
probably already know this—that's if you can see us all
down here still makin' fools of ourselves—but Jack thinks
it's Kristen. You know, leavin' the postcards. And hell, I
guess it very well could be. I'd ask her, but there's a part of
me that doesn't want to spoil your secret. So, I tell you what,
buddy. I just won't ask."*

*I stop talkin' for a few minutes and listen as the freight
train passes in the distance. It roars and clanks and then
roars some more, and then it's quiet again.*

*"But...," I go on, "at the same time, it would be nice to
know someday who she is. You know, if you wanted to tell
me," I add.*

*My gaze slowly wanders to his stone and the indented
letters that spell his name—*Owen Katz. *And I sit there
thinkin' about him and thinkin' about Ashley and wishin'
these two could have met.*

*"I think you would have liked her. She's elegant and
proper and all that, but she's also got this free-spirit thing
goin' on. I guess you could say, she's like Kate Middleton
and Kate Hudson all wrapped into one—if you can imagine
that."*

*I let the space around us grow quiet then, so quiet that I
can hear the squirrel scamperin' in the tree next to us. It's*

106

really a small graveyard. I never see anyone else here. But I know people come. There's two beer cans sittin' next to Owen; Jack's been here again. And of course, there's the postcard. I laugh to myself. I guess I could set up a stakeout. Then I'd find out who's been leavin' these cards. But then again, somethin' tells me Owen will let me know when he wants me to know...and not a minute sooner.

After a little while longer of just sittin' and thinkin', I hear the first of the cicadas startin' their evening cry, remindin' me it's gettin' late.

"Well, buddy, I guess I better be takin' off," I say, pushin' up from the little stool. "I'll see ya when I see ya."

I stand there and look at the postcard one last time. I know next time I come here, this one will be gone and another one will be in its place. I wonder where he's goin' next. Paris? Sydney? Naples?

I push the milking seat closer to Owen and squeeze my cap back over my head. Then I tip my bill to Mr. Katz and start my slow trek back to the old, iron gates that flank the entrance to the little cemetery.

Chapter Eighteen

Present

Rem

I get out of my truck and make my way to the mailbox. It wasn't a hard day at work, just a long day. When computers decide to crap out on ya, and when all you deal with is computers, that makes for a fun day.

Inside the box, I find a couple envelopes—all junk mail—and a small package. I grab it all but look at the package first. There's no return address on it. There's just my address written front and center in black marker.

I tuck the junk mail under my arm and make my way back up the driveway. And in the meantime, I try to rip the box open with my hands first, but that doesn't work. So, I grab my keychain and use my house key to cut through the tape. That works.

I wrestle the tape away and finally loosen one of the cardboard sides. And when I peek inside, I notice a book.

My feet immediately stop flat on the little white rocks, and my heart comes damn near close to doin' the same thing. At the top of the book is a name, but not just any name. It's *her* name, *Ashley Westcott*—in big, bold, capitalized letters. And under her name, there's a title. *Worth It.*

I take a second to look at the cover. There's a guy and a girl on it. She's on a swing. He looks as if he's pushin' her. I pull back the cover and finally feel a smile pushin' past my lips. *Wow! She did it.*

I glance over the first page, and immediately, my eyes stop and come to rest on some familiar handwriting:

Rem,
Was it?

Was it? I turn the page to see if there's anything written on the back or the next page. *Was it? Was it what?*

There's nothin' else. Just the question. I close the book and look at the cover again. It's her name, all right. I flip it over and notice her photo on the back. It says she lives in Lakeway, has a dog named Tiger and is working on her next novel. She looks the same in the photo as she did at Hall's—the last time I saw her. And she looks just as beautiful as the first day I met her.

Well, I'll be. She did it. She wrote a book—a real book. It feels a little weird to be proud of her, but I am.

My eyes skim the back and follow over the text. The words say it's a book about a girl who fell in love with a boy and the boy who broke her heart.

I finish reading over the words, and then it slowly sinks in.

"Oh, shit."

Chapter Nineteen

Past (1.5 Years Earlier)

Ashley

"You sure there's a big city out this way?" Rem asks, looking out the window.

We've been driving for the last forty-five minutes in Iowa. And there hasn't been much more than fields the entire time.

"Patience, my dear," I say, catching his gaze for a moment. He looks so cute sitting over there in the passenger's seat. I feel as if he doesn't exactly know what to do when he hasn't got a steering wheel in front of him. For the first half hour of our trip, he worked on my glove compartment. About a year ago, I stuffed the car's manual in there and got it stuck. For the last year, I haven't been able to open the compartment door. But that changed today—the *first day that Remington Jude had to sit in my passenger's seat for more than five minutes.*

The next project he tackled was my side mirror. Evidently, it wasn't in the right position. He spouted off something about corners and then asked me to look into it every couple seconds.

The last project was his seat. It's at the perfect height and angle now, apparently. And now, I guess he's run out of things to do.

"You know," I say, regaining his attention. "I've never actually brought a guy home before."

He tears his stare from the window to look at me.

"Like ever?"

I shake my head. "Like ever," I repeat.

"Well, damn it."

"What?" I ask.

"Well, now your parents are gonna be expectin' this perfect guy, who's like thirty and works for Microsoft and drives a Porsche or somethin'."

"What?" I start to laugh. "Why would they expect that?"

"I don't know. That's who I would expect you to bring home. And I, damn sure, wouldn't expect some country kid from Ava, Missouri, who drives a pickup truck."

"Then, you must not know me very well, Remington Jude. Because I'd much prefer the pickup-truck boy from Ava over the Microsoft-Porsche guy, who probably wears too much gel in his hair."

He looks over at me and smiles.

"Ashley Westcott, you're too good for me."

"I know," I say, with a wide grin.

"P.S., I don't wear ANY gel in my hair."

I look over at him. He's got this serious expression plastered to his face. "I know. That's why I like you."

He reaches over then and pulls my closest hand away from the steering wheel. "I can't wait to meet your family,"

112

he says, kissing the top of my fingers, then cradling my hand in his.

"They'll love you," I promise. "And your gel-free hair."

He just gives me a satisfied grin and then goes back to looking out his window again. And all I can think is: How did I ever get so lucky to find this man?

Once we get into Omaha, traffic is traffic—bumper to bumper for several miles, but then it's fine. We pull up into the driveway, and I can tell he's nervous. But I can also tell he's excited. He's got this look in his eyes he gets when a big game is about to start or when I agree to do something like mushroom hunting with him. I can tell he's excited, and that makes me happy.

"So, my little sister, Lana, came home for the weekend to meet you," I say. "She goes to the University of Nebraska, and she's got a little bit of a hippie thing going on, just to warn you."

"A what?"

"Hippie. You know? My mom thinks it's just a phase, but I don't think it's a phase."

"Oh... I don't think I've ever met a real hippie," he says, looking a little panicked. His little scared face makes me laugh. It looks cute on him.

"Don't worry," I say. "She loves everyone."

"Okay," he whispers. The big breath he takes doesn't go unnoticed.

"Seriously," I say, "you have nothing to worry about." He seems to relax a little.

"Oh, and did I mention my dad is a former Marine?"

"What?" He almost shouts the word.

"Kidding," I say.

"Damn, girl," he mumbles, lowering his head. "You're

tryin' to kill me; I know it."

I just laugh and get out of the car. And when I meet him on the passenger's side, I grab his hand.

Immediately, he looks down at our hands. "Do you think we should hold hands?" he asks.

"Rem!"

"Well, I don't know! I'm still not convinced your dad's not somethin' mean and big, and I'm not really sure if I should be more afraid of him or your sister."

I try to choke down my amusement, as I kiss him on the cheek. "It's my mom you should be afraid of," I whisper into his ear.

He gives me this terrified look, and it's absolutely priceless—definitely worth scaring the hell out of him for no reason.

We get inside, and I set my purse down onto the floor next to a bunch of shoes. And almost instantly, the sweet scent of cinnamon fills my nose. I must be home. My parents' house has been infused with the smell of cinnamon ever since my sister mentioned to my mom one day that the scent can help improve brain function. That was almost three years ago. Now, I can't smell cinnamon without thinking of home.

"Mom," I say. "We're here."

"Ashley!" My sister comes running into the hall and throws her arms around me and then, without so much as a hesitation or an introduction, for that matter, she throws her arms around Rem, too.

"You have a good aura," she says, pulling away from Rem. "I can feel it."

Rem just smiles and nods. I can tell he doesn't know what to say...or do.

"That's a good thing," my sister says.

"Okay," he says, nodding, but still not completely convinced—I can tell.

"Lana," I say, smiling, "this is Rem."

114

"Remmm...?" she hums, drawing out the last letter of his name. "Is that short for something?"

"Remington," Rem replies.

"Good," she says. "Can I call you Remington then?"

Rem glances at me and then smiles at Lana. "Sure, if you'd like."

Lana bobs her head once. "I think I would like." And with that, she dances away—like literally twirls into the next room—while Rem leans over and whispers in my ear: "Did she say I smell good?"

"Yeah," I say, smiling, "something like that."

"Sweetheart, dinner is almost ready." My mom suddenly appears in the hallway and kisses me on the cheek before she turns to Rem. "And you must be the boy we've heard so much about."

Rem looks at me and gives me a pleased grin before he looks back at my mom. "Hi, Miss Westcott." He holds out his hand. My mom shakes it.

My dad says that you can tell a lot about a person by his or her handshake. Thus, new people always get handshakes in our house.

"Mom, this is Rem," I say.

"Well, it's nice to meet you, Rem."

Rem just nods and smiles. He looks shy, but also somehow, confident, at the same time. I think that's what I like about him so much. He's always two things at once. For example, he can't just be sweet. He's got to be sweet and sexy. Like when he tells me I'm beautiful, it's always in a whisper or a raspy tone with a hungry look in his eyes. Or like, even when he's upset, he wears this face that somehow says: I won't give up on you.

"Why don't you guys come into the dining room." My mother's voice rings through my ears, breaking up my thoughts.

I smile at Rem. "They love you," I whisper into his ear. I notice his shoulders seem to relax a little right before I take

*his hand and lead him into the next room. My dad is in there,
setting a bowl of cooked carrots onto the table.*

"Dad," I say, "this is Rem."

*"Hello," my dad says, brushing his hands together,
before holding one out to Rem.*

Rem takes his hand and shakes it.

"It's nice to meet you, son," Dad says.

*Rem smiles kindly. And I don't miss the inconspicuous
nod my dad gives me, either. He's done the same thing all
my life. Every person he shakes hands with, he either nods or
doesn't. It's his way of letting me know who's "okay" and
who's "not okay." A nod means:* this person can be
trusted. *No nod:* I don't ever want you alone in the same
room with this person. *I know the drill, and I breathe a
sigh of relief when I get the nod, even if it is just a formality
for me. I already trust Remington Jude, and I don't think
there's anything in this world that can convince me
otherwise.*

*We all sit down shortly after that. I take a seat; Rem
takes the seat next to me. My sister sits across from us, and
my parents sit at either ends of the table.*

*While we eat, my parents quiz Rem on everything from
where he lives to what TV programming he watches. My
dad's got this thing with TV shows, too. If you watch sports
or the History channel, you're okay in his book. If you say
you watch anything else, he automatically puts you on a list
with all the other people he's not so sure about yet. Rem said
he watches a lot of sports, so I guess he passed that test.*

*"Remington?" my sister says, once there's a pause in
the conversation. She speaks in her usual soft and thoughtful
tone.*

Rem looks up from his plate in mid-chew.

"What direction does your house face?"

"Sorry?" he says to her.

"Do you live in a house?" she asks.

"Uh, yeah," Rem stutters.

"What direction does it face?" she asks again.

My mom rolls her eyes and smiles. My dad acts as if he doesn't hear the question. I think he believes that if he doesn't "hear" it, it wasn't actually said. Neither of my parents has fully bought into her lifestyle, yet.

"Oh, uh, east, I believe," Rem says.

"Good." Lana nods and then goes back to chewing on her raw carrot.

"Good," Rem simply repeats, with a smile.

We make it through the dinner without any casualties. And afterward, Lana heads up to her room. My dad retires with my mom to the living room. And I lead Rem out to the back porch.

"You made it," I say.

"I made it," he echoes.

I sit down on a padded bench, and he joins me.

"You think they liked me?"

I find his stare. It's getting dark all around us now, but I can still see that beautiful sea in his eyes. "I think they loved you," I say.

"Your sister's cool."

I nod. "She's a lot like my grandmother—the one that taught us about the bamboo plants."

"Yeah," he says, as if he's remembering. "I can see that. And I bet your sister has one of those love plants, too."

I laugh. "She does. But hers isn't so much a love plant. It has ten stalks and means completion."

"Aah," he says, tilting his head back slightly. "That sounds fitting. But that has to be one hell of a big plant."

"It is," I agree. "It takes up, like, her whole desk upstairs."

He chuckles a little at that. "Come here," he says then, pulling me closer.

I fall into his chest. He's warm, and he smells like his cologne. I love his smell.

"So, this is where you grew up?" he asks.

"Yeah," I say. "There's a park not too far from here where I spent a lot of my summers. In fact, I got my first broken arm when I fell off the monkey bars there."

"Your first?"

I nod. "Yeah, I broke it again in junior high in a softball game. And don't ask me how. I was sliding one second, and then the next, I felt this sharp pain, and all of a sudden, it was Broken Arm Número Dos." I hold out two fingers.

"Wow," he exclaims. "You really are tough."

I just laugh into his chest.

"Which one?" he asks.

"My right." I hold up my right arm, and he takes it and trails soft kisses from my elbow to my wrist. The feel of his lips on my skin sends a rush of heat to my face. I try to hide it by burying my face deeper into the muscles in his chest.

"And my high school is about a mile down the road," I say, after his last kiss to my arm.

"Do you think you would have noticed me in high school?" he asks.

I look up at him and into his eyes. "I don't know how I couldn't have."

"Even if I would have just been a sophomore when you were a senior..."

"I still would have noticed you."

"We could have been high school sweethearts," he says.

"We would have been," I say, laughin' softly to myself. "I really didn't have a high school sweetheart."

"Really?"

"Nope," I confirm.

"That surprises me."

"Well, you've never met the boys in my high school."

"Touché," he says.

He runs the inside of his hand gently along the length of my arm. The contrast of my skin and his rougher skin works to soothe me somehow.

"Well, I didn't have a high school sweetheart, either," he says, squeezing me closer. *"I had too many knuckleheads in my life advisin' me against it."*

"Nooo," I say, sarcastically.

"I know it's hard to believe," he says. I can feel the laugh tunneling through his chest, even before it leaves his lips.

Then, he grows quiet, and I just try to soak up everything about this night, including the way my dad laughed at his jokes and how my mom smiled at him. They see what I see, too. And what I see is only the beginning of how much I feel for this boy.

"Ashley?"

"Hmm?" I peek up at him, not wanting to lift my face from his chest.

"This is one of my new favorite moments."

I smile wide. "Rem?"

"Yeah?"

"I'm happy you're here."

I hear him breathe in and then out, and I feel his chest rise and fall as he does it. "Me too," he says. *"Me too."*

And with that, I nuzzle deeper into his muscles and feel his arms wrap tighter around me. In this moment, I can't remember what it's like to hurt. It feels so far away now. Now, everything just seems so happy and so full of life and love and possibility. I want to hold onto this feeling for dear life. I don't ever want to feel what it's like to lose it. I don't ever want to feel what it's like to lose Remington Jude. I'm falling for him. I know that I am.

I'm falling for Remington Jude.

Chapter Twenty

Past

Ashley

"Remington." I sing his name because I think he secretly likes when I do it.

"What, baby?"

I come up behind him and throw my arms around his neck. "Don't work today," I whisper into his ear. "Stay home and play with me." I kiss his clean-shaven cheek and squeeze his shoulders tighter.

He swings around in his chair, and I fall into his lap. "We can take a walk along the river or go to your grandpa's farm...or build a bonfire and invite the whole town over."

He cringes at that last one, and it makes me laugh. "Or...," I say, "we can just snuggle on the couch all day and watch old movies."

"I think..." he says, standing up and taking me with

him. I playfully squeal and throw my arms around his neck as he slides one arm under my legs and one behind my back and carries me toward the living room.

He lies me down onto the couch and kisses my forehead. "I think that last one's my favorite," he says, falling gently on top of me. His mouth hovers over mine. I can feel his warm breaths tenderly hit my lips one by one. "I love you, Ashley Westcott."

My smile starts to fade. Something in me stings at my heart a little. I haven't heard those words in a long time. But I look into his eyes, and I see him; I see the man who is familiar, who is sexy, who is love, who is mine.

"I..." I place a hand on either side of his suntanned face. "I love you, too, Remington Jude."

At my words, his lips edge up.

"I should have said that a long time ago, shouldn't I have?" he asks.

I can't help but smile. "I wouldn't have believed you a day sooner."

He looks at me with this longing that I don't think I'll ever get enough of. It makes me feel as if I'm the only girl in the world for him.

"And," he says, reaching into his pocket and pulling out a little, silver key, "I want you to have this."

"What?" I ask, taking it into my hand.

"It's my spare key."

"To here? To your house?"

He just nods, and I feel my smile growing wider.

"You know, Ashley Westcott," he says, in a low, rasping voice. The way he says my name makes me take notice. "I realize there was probably a chance—before we ever met—that our paths were never gonna cross in this life." He shrugs his shoulders a little. "You know, maybe it was some choice we made or didn't make that caused a road to fork a different way or somethin', and we missed each other by just an inch. We'd never know it, of course, and

we'd go on livin' our lives in blissful ignorance, never knowin' what we missed out on. ...I don't know, maybe we'd each marry different people and have a couple kids. And maybe we'd grow old with the people we married." He pauses and lowers his eyes before finding mine again. "But I know, if that were the case—if I never would have crossed paths with you—I never would have known love. Because as far as I'm concerned, there's only one definition of it out there...and I'm convinced it's lyin' right here next to me."

He says his last word, and then he leans in and presses his lips to mine. "Did you know that?" he asks, pulling away from my lips and trailing tender kisses down my neck.

I can't even form a word. There are tears in my eyes, as if they're literally welling up from somewhere deep inside my soul, and his kisses are making me melt into a pool of sweet dizziness under his body. And with one last kiss onto my collarbone, he wraps his arms around me and pulls me close. I feel so safe as he holds me in this happy silence. And before long, I hear him hum a soft tune near my ear. I recognize it. It's the song we first danced to. It's the song we were listening to when I think we both knew we were in for a long ride. I squeeze the key into the palm of my hand, and then I nuzzle my cheek deep into his chest, and I breathe him in. I love this man. And I know, in this moment and without a doubt, I was right about this place and in coming here. To me, Ava was the fork in the road. This place has both healed my soul and stolen my heart. Thank God for this small town. And thank God that Remington Jude calls it home.

Chapter Twenty-One

Present

"Hey, Jack," I mumble. My mind feels distracted, like it's somewhere else entirely.

"Hey, Rem! Pull up a seat." He says the words way too cheerfully.

I throw my jacket over an old wooden chair across from him. And right before I take a seat, I steal a quick glance around the little bar, checkin' to see who's here. "Thanks for meetin' me here," I say.

"No problem. So, what's up?"

I lean into the table. There's no one in the bar except Old Man Seeger, who can't even hear, but I don't take any chances. "Well, you know how we joked about her writing a book one day?"

Jack's quiet for a second. Then he cocks his head to one side. "Uh, yeah?"

"Well..." I draw out the word.

He doesn't move. He just narrows an eye at me. "Wait, what are you sayin'?"

I can feel a long, drawn-out breath drag across my lips, as he stares back at me. "I'm sayin' she wrote a book."

"Ashley?"

"Yeah," I say.

"About you?"

"Well, not exactly. But it's a little too familiar, if you know what I mean." I look around the bar again before my eyes settle back on him.

"Wow." He says the word like it's all still settin' in. Then he leans back until both of the chair's front legs are off the floor. "Wow," he says again.

I sit back in my own chair and just watch him shake his head.

"It's you, you know?" he says.

I shrug my shoulders and open my mouth to counter that statement, but nothin' comes out.

"Well...?" he asks.

"Well, what?"

"Well, what'd she say?"

I rub the back of my neck. "I don't know. What do you mean?"

"I mean, what does she say about you?"

"I don't know. I just read a few chapters. The book was in my mailbox last night when I got home." I don't tell him I stopped readin' it because it was hittin' too close to home. I don't tell him that I got scared; I leave that part out.

Jack stares up at the little bar's ceiling as if it's the

most interesting thing in the world. "Wow," he exclaims again, still shakin' his head. He does that for a little while longer, until his eyes eventually settle back on mine. "You've gotta finish that book."

I push out some air I think I had been holdin' hostage in my lungs.

"Seriously, what are you doin' here?" he asks. "Go finish it."

"I just... Well, so what?"

He looks at me with both corners of his mouth turned down at the ends. "What? What do mean, *so what*?"

"So what if she wrote it?" I ask. "So what if it sounds familiar? So what?"

"So what?" He gives me this look as if I just spoke a bunch of gibberish. Then, he rests the chair's legs back onto the floor and leans in over the table. "It's your life, dude. If it's real in the beginnin', the end's gotta be real too, right? Or at least, it's gotta be what she wants to be real. Right?" Now, he scoots his chair even closer and rests his elbows on the table. "Don't you wanna know what she thinks? Don't you wanna know the ending? I mean, she just up and left. Just like that. Aren't you curious to know why?"

I sit there and think about what he's sayin' for a minute. Then I slowly shake my head. "No," I say.

"Come on, man. You gotta read it." He swipes his hand at me and sits back in his chair.

"I don't wanna know."

"But it's your life, dude."

"That's ridiculous."

"Is it?" he asks. He takes a long drag of his beer and then sets it back down onto the table.

I let out an audible sigh, mostly because I don't know

what to say next. It sounds crazy, but maybe he's got a point. What if the book is meant to be a message? But what? What could it possibly say that would change anything?

I shake my head. "No," I say.

"What? What do you mean *no?*

"No, I'm not readin' it."

He looks at me as if he wants to ask me *why*, but he never does.

"Who says I have to read the damn thing?" I ask.

His elbows are back on the table. "Dude, let me put it to you like this." He rests a finger on his chin. "See, it's like somebody just gave you a time machine and a crystal ball, and you're not even tempted to look into either one of 'em? ...At all?"

I shake my head. "I'd rather not see it all played out again, and I'd rather not know how it ends right now, either. I'll figure it out eventually anyway."

Jack sucks in a long, deep breath before crossin' his arms over his chest. "Fair enough." He seems to have conceded. "Okay. You don't have to read the book. But you can't keep this whole, damn town from readin' it. And you know once they catch wind of it, they'll want to get their hands on it quicker than flies to shit."

This time, I'm the one restin' my elbows on the table. I put my hands to my mouth, and I sit there, playin' it all out it in my head. Then, finally, I press my back against the back of the chair, and I shrug. "Let them read it." I try to say it with as much indifference as I can, even though just the thought of the entire, damn town knowin' the whole story scares the hell out of me.

"So, you're okay with them knowin' how your story went...how it ends?"

A burnin' starts to burrow through my chest. It sits

heavy on my lungs, and then it takes over my throat and makes it hard to breathe. "As far as I'm concerned, the Rem and Ashley story ended the moment she left," I say.

And at that, I get up, grab my jacket and head for the door before the burnin' can hit my eyes, too. But just before I can get my hand on the screen door's frame, I hear Jack's voice loud and clear behind me—though I wish I hadn't.

"And as far as she's concerned?"

I stop.

"And it ended that same moment—as far as she's concerned?" he says again, a little less rushed this time.

I pretend to ignore his last words, and I storm out of the bar. Jack knows not to push me on this. It's the only thing that makes me break.

Chapter Twenty-Two

Past (1.5 Years Earlier)

Ashley

"Do you hear that?"

"Hear what?" I ask.

"The cicadas. They're crying," Rem whispers.

I listen. And as if it's for the first time—even though I know it's not—I hear them. I hear the loud vibrations of their wings beating like trains rushing down a track. The sound is continuous, a continuous stream of echoes and beats. And when you focus on it, it almost becomes deafening.

"Why are they crying?" I ask, whispering near his ear.

He sits back against the wooden porch railing, and I, by default, fall deeper into the little place he's made for me between his arms and legs—the little place I've grown accustomed to possessing.

"Because they know..." He stops for a moment. His words are low and fragile, like a poem or a sad song. But I stay silent as the cicadas' cries slowly engulf us. And I wait. I've heard this sad song before.

"Because they know immortality...yet not eternal youth," he continues.

I look up at him, and his light eyes catch on mine. At the same time, he tucks a strand of my hair behind my ear. I love it when he does that.

"They cry because we have what they want: To be mortal," he recites. "See, there was once this Greek god named Tithonus, and he loved the Greek goddess, Aurora. And one day, Aurora asked Zeus to make Tithonus immortal just like her, so they could live together forever. But she forgot one thing." He presses his lips to my cheek. "She forgot to ask for eternal youth for Tithonus as well," he whispers low and near my ear. "And so, Tithonus grew old and lived forever bound by the chains of old age. And eventually, old Tithonus turned into a cicada and spent the rest of eternity despising his immortality."

I let a couple moments pass, feeling the warmth of a sunny day gone by lightly pushing over our faces.

"Where'd you hear that?" I eventually ask.

"What?"

"The story?" I say, a little too breathy, a little too moved.

"Oh." He seems to think about it. "I don't know. That story is probably as old as this town. I can't even think of a time I didn't know it. Everyone around here knows it."

"Oh," I say, feeling my shoulders relax again.

"It's just a story. Don't worry, I don't believe it; I'm not crazy."

"No, I know," I say, smiling again. "I like the story." I take a breath and reach up and run my fingers through his dark hair. I don't tell him I've heard it before. I just close my eyes and let my head fall back against his strong chest, and I

listen to the cicadas' sad cries.

"I think I'd take immortality even if it meant I wouldn't stay young forever," I say, after a moment. "I think I'd just be happy knowing that I could be with the one I love forever."

"That sounds nice," he says, wrapping his arms around my ribs and pressing his lips to the top of my head. "But the thing is, we have breath in our lungs and joy in our hearts and time on our minds. ...See, we don't have forever; therefore, every moment is precious. Every moment means somethin'."

I replay his words in my head. I want to believe them. They sound so beautiful tonight. But I know as well as any that if I lost him tomorrow, I would still be wishing for eternity with him. I love him so much. It's like I can feel him in my bones. It's as if I can feel him becoming a part of me, a part of my DNA. I love him. I love that he's not afraid to walk around with my name written on his heart for everyone to see. I love that he makes me laugh—that he says things like, I'll be and damn near. I love how confident he is, yet how shy and awkward he can be, too—and often times, in the same breath. And I love that he loves his family and his friends. I know he'd do anything for them, and it makes me believe he'd do anything for me, too. And I know it sounds simple, but he also makes me feel...wanted. No matter if I'm wearing dirty cowboy boots or five-inch heels, he acts as if he just can't get enough of me. And what girl doesn't want that? He's a surprising human really. And I thought I'd met Forever in the past, but it turns out, Forever was waiting for me all along in a little town called Ava.

Chapter Twenty-Three

Present

Rem

I'm at my kitchen table. It's Saturday afternoon, and I haven't left this room all day. Her book is in my hands. I picked up where I first left off before I had the talk with Jack. I think I knew all along that I'd read this book as fast as I could. I think I just wanted Jack to tell me not to. I wanted him to tell me it was okay to not want to hear how my story ends. But of course, Jack didn't do that. And deep down, I knew he wouldn't. So, here I am, watchin' the pages of my life unfold through two characters I only met a couple days ago. Some parts are hard to read. I try to skim over those words as fast as I can. But other parts, I read more than once, like the part when they go mushroom huntin' for the first time, or the time they have their first kiss near that black river. And I think I read the part where he asked her to dance that very first night no less than four times.

Then, all too soon, I get to the last page, and I turn it. And my eyes immediately go to followin' over the final few sentences in the book:

I know it's not supposed to be painless. I know all that matters is that it was worth it—that it was worth the white scars we carved into each other's hearts, that it was worth the story we so painfully, yet happily, etched, in our own handwriting, onto the fragile surface of our souls.

But was it worth it? Was it worth it, knowing that now, you and I will be marked in eternity? Was it worth it, knowing that someday, the angels will see our hearts, and they will read our souls, and they will know? They will know that we once shared this life—that on this earth, though we walked apart, our hearts and our souls walked side by side.

Yes, I know; it isn't supposed to be painless. Love isn't supposed to be painless. It's supposed to be worth it. But all I wonder still is: Was it worth it? Was it worth all the pain? Was it all worth it...to you?

I turn the page.

The End.

I read the last two words before slowly closin' the book. And for a long time, I just stare at the white wall in front of me. I think I'm expectin' somethin' to happen. I'm half expectin' the wall to move or for her to come through it, as if she had been watchin' me read the pages of our life this entire time. Or maybe I'm expectin' my world to crash in on me or to wake up and realize everything I once knew is all just a dream or some well-written story. But none of that happens. None. Of. It.

So, instead, I just sit here and stare at the wall, while every one of my veins and every one of my bones and every inch of my mind fills up with the words: *Was it all worth it...to you?*

Chapter Twenty-Four

Present

Rem

"Okay, what's up? What did you want? I had to put clothes on for this. And I couldn't find any clean boxers, so I'm also goin' commando under these old sweats here, so..."

I stop him right there. "Jeez, no thanks for the visual there, dude," I say.

He takes a seat in the chair across from me. Hall's is quiet. It's the usual Sunday night. The juke box is playin' some old song, but other than that, there's not a soul makin' a noise.

"I read it."

That's all I say. And then I sit back and watch his face go from tired and apathetic to a damn, lit-up

Christmas tree.

"Well, what'd she say?"

"Now, you boys aren't up to any trouble, are ya?" Kristen sets a bottle down in front of Jack.

Jack slips his elbows onto the table and smiles up at her. "Now, when have I ever been up to trouble?" he asks.

"Last week, you were drag racin' that Fischer boy from Tipton," she says, with her hands on her hips.

Jack just looks at her with amazement written all over his face. "I swear, girl, you know me like a book you read a thousand times. Why aren't we married already?"

Kristen rolls her eyes and sets her gaze on me. And not even a second after lookin' at me, she cocks her head to the side. "You're talkin' about Ashley, aren't you?"

I narrow my eyes at her. "What?"

She turns to Jack. "Every time he wears that face, it's her name I'm hearin'." She directs her attention back over to me. "It's really no secret, sweetheart."

"All right, you got us," Jack says, throwin' up his hands.

"Damn it, Jack," I say, droppin' my eyes and shakin' my head.

"Don't worry, baby," Kristen says, layin' her hand on my shoulder. "I already knew it."

She leaves us then, and I just frown at Jack.

"She never calls me *sweetheart...or baby*," Jack says, his eyes followin' after her.

I ignore him because he's apparently ignorin' me. And hell, I don't talk about Ashley, and I definitely don't talk about her enough to have a "face."

"Hey, Kris, you got any food still back there?" Jack calls out to Kristen.

"Kitchen's closed," she shouts over her shoulder.

"Anything?" he begs.

It's quiet then, and his eyes eventually land back on me. "Okay, so you read it?"

"Yeah," I say, nodding. "She or Jen ends up..."

"Jen?"

"Yeah, the main character," I say. "Her name is Jen. But anyway, she ends up..."

Kristen comes back and tosses a bag of chips onto the table.

Jack looks at Kristen with what looks as if it's adoration, but I can't tell whether it's sarcastic or real. "I love it when you cook for me, baby," he says.

Kristen waves her hand and rolls her eyes. "Yeah, yeah. Don't eat 'em too fast. That's all you're gettin'."

Jack tears into the bag, throws his head back and empties half the chips into his mouth. Meanwhile, Kristen turns to me. "You know, you fly too close to the sun."

I laugh. It might sound nervous, but it's a laugh, all the same. "What's that supposed to mean?"

"It means you play with fire, you're gonna get burned."

"Damn it, girl." I laugh some more. "Quit speakin' in riddles."

She smiles and shrugs her shoulders. "Look, I don't know what happened between the two of you. All I know is that she left. And don't get me wrong. I loved Ashley, and I don't understand why the two of you aren't together. I always pictured you gettin' married and havin' babies. I even had a dress picked out for the wedding ceremony." She pauses before continuing. "But if she hurt you, Rem, she's fire, and you should just let it be."

"Kristen," I say, "Ashley's not fire...at least, not in that way."

Jack quickly makes eye contact with me and gives me

136

a proud smile, and we both chuckle under our breath.

"Rem, there is no other way. Fire is fire," she says, with a soft smile.

A heavy sigh involuntarily replaces my grin. Sometimes, I wish they all knew the story. They all suspect I'm innocent here, and I'm not. And I'd be happy to set them all straight, but Ashley didn't even want me to know her secret, so I just don't feel right tellin' it to anyone.

"Thanks for the talk, Kris," I say.

"Mm-hmm," she hums, grabbin' a can of salt off the bar top. I watch her as she goes to fillin' up the little white bottle on a table two down from ours.

"All I'm sayin' is that when your past calls, don't answer," she says. "It's got nothin' new to say."

I laugh again, but it's not sincere. I know one thing: She hasn't talked to my past lately.

I tip the bill of my cap in her direction and return my attention to Jack, who's just finished off the bag of chips.

"Does she have a quote book back there or somethin'?" I ask.

"Probably," he says, not at all fazed. "Okay, so what's the verdict?"

"The book doesn't end."

"What?"

I shake my head. "It doesn't end."

"How can it not end? Don't all books end?"

I feel my shoulders shrug. "Not this one. I mean, they don't get back together, but they don't *not* get back together, either."

"Hmm." He sits back and gnaws on his bottom lip.

"But she signed it," I say.

He looks at me as if he doesn't understand. "Okay?"

"She signed it with: *Was it?*"

"Was it?" he repeats.

I nod.

He raises his shoulders and gives me a puzzled look. "Was it, what?"

"Well, I didn't know what she was talkin' about when I first looked at it. But then I got to the last page, and right before the book ends, Jen—the girl—asks the guy if it was worth it—if it was worth bein' with her. And as far as I can tell, that's the only question in the book like it."

Jack's eyes grow big, and I can tell he takes a quick, even breath. "Wow," he says, noddin' his head. "Are you supposed to answer that?"

I shake my head and sigh. "I don't know."

"Wait, why is she askin' you that? I mean, you clearly loved her, and if you loved her, it was at least worth *a go*, right? So why is that even a question she'd be askin'?"

I don't say anything.

"You did." He cocks his head. "You did love her? Right, Rem?"

I nod. "Yeah. Yeah, of course."

"But how could she not know that? You two were like freakin' Johnny and June or somethin'. There isn't one person in this town that doesn't know you loved..." He stops. "No, wait a minute. Let me start over." He holds up a finger. "There isn't one person in this town that doesn't know you *still love* Ashley Westcott."

I don't say anything. I just go to gnawin' on the inside of my cheek.

"But her," he adds, sittin' back even further in his chair. "Everyone knows but her," he says again.

Silent moments tick out between us.

"That's it, isn't it?" He shakes his head. "Why is that, Rem?" His look has turned accusing all of a sudden.

138

I take a deep breath and then force it out just as fast as I got it in. Then I look around the bar. Kristen's in the far corner now, still fillin' up those little white bottles with salt. She's not in earshot, and there's no one else in the bar. I put my hand to my mouth, hold it there for a second and then let it drop to the surface of the table. All the while, Jack's got this stare on me as if he's preparin' for what I'm about to say. And maybe he should be.

"What did you do, Rem?"

I shake my head and stare at a tiny hole in the table's wooden surface. "I didn't *do* anything."

Jack sighs.

"It's what I *said* right before she left," I confess.

"Wait a minute. So you know why she left?"

I don't answer him. I figure that's answer enough.

"This whole time...," he goes on. "This whole, damn time that we're all sittin' here wonderin' why this girl just turned in her keys, closed her bank account and left town, you knew why?" He pauses to push out an exhausted-soundin' sigh. "Rem, what did you say?"

I look up at the ceiling and squeeze my eyes shut for a brief moment. "I told her I never loved her."

"What?" He practically shouts it. My eyes snap open, and at the same time, Kristen's gaze cuts in our direction. I lift my hand and shake my head to let her know it's fine. It seems to work because she goes back to doin' what she was doin'.

"What?" Jack says again, as if I didn't hear him the first time. Thankfully, this time, he doesn't shout it.

"I was mad. And she was lookin' for a reason to run. I just thought I'd give it to her."

"What?" He runs his hand through his hair, looks around and then fixes his eyes back on me. "Why? Why were you mad? And why was she lookin' for a reason to run?"

I try to laugh, as I haphazardly shrug my shoulders. "That's the million-dollar question in this town, isn't it?"

"Damn it, Rem!"

He's getting impatient now.

"I'm like your best friend. Aren't I supposed to know this stuff? Best friends are supposed to know shit that no one else knows about you, right?"

I breathe out and just stare at him for a second. I really don't know why I never told him. I know he would have kept Ashley's secret. But then again, I've never told anyone. Of course, nobody's ever really asked, either. Either they're too damn scared or they just like believin' their own versions of the truth better than the truth.

"What did she do?" he asks.

My eyes fall on Kristen in the corner again. They stay there for a few seconds. I watch her spill some salt onto the table. She takes a pinch and throws it over her shoulder. Then she brushes the rest of it onto the floor. I notice the clock next. It's just a simple black and white office clock, set fifteen minutes fast, hangin' on a tan, wallpapered wall that otherwise would be empty. The second hand on it ticks out several, rhythmic beats before my eyes fall onto a rerun of an old game on the small TV above us. Then there's nothin' left. There's nothin' left to help me avoid his question.

"She was in love with someone else," I say, under my breath.

Both his eyes narrow, but he doesn't say anything at first.

My heart is racin', but somehow, there's this calm that flows through my veins. I've never said that out loud.

"She cheated on you?" He looks as if he can barely get the words out.

"No," I quickly say. "No, she didn't cheat."

Thin lines appear on his forehead. "Then what in the hell are you talkin' about?" he asks.

I fold my arms across my chest and look for the answer on the ceiling. Then after a few moments, I level my gaze back on Jack. "Owen," I say. "She was in love with Owen."

Jack might as well have seen a ghost. His face goes completely white, and his jaw hangs slack.

"How?" he asks.

I feel my cheeks puff up before I forcefully push the air past my lips. "Before she moved here. In Minnesota. At school."

Understanding seems to, all of a sudden, wash over him. His hand is loosely rested up against his mouth now. Otherwise, he's as stiff as a board, his eyes planted on somethin' across the bar, until his gaze darts back to me. "The postcards?"

I just nod my head. "It was her."

"Wow," he says, seemingly takin' it all in, piece by piece—just like I had to a year ago. "Wow, I'm sorry, buddy. That...I didn't see comin'."

I sit back and let out a long sigh. "Yeah," I say, "well, neither did I."

Chapter Twenty-Five

Past (1 Year Earlier)

Rem

I purposefully place the ring box open with the ring inside of it onto the coffee table box. Ashley's in Nebraska visiting her family, so I know she won't walk in and see it.

"Big game tonight," I hear Jack yell from the hallway.

My heart races as I frantically make sure he'll easily be able to see the little box. It feels like the year I got a train set for Christmas. I'm so damn excited I can barely contain my six-year-old self.

I carefully step away from the box, run to my chair and jump into it. Then I rest my ankle on my opposite knee and try to look casual, while I search for the power button on the remote.

"Oh." He looks at me startled when he enters the room. "You're in here. When your dumb ass didn't answer, I thought you were out back."

I shake my head. "No, been here the whole time."

"Then why are you being so damn quiet?"

"No reason," I say.

"What's wrong with you?"

"What?" I laugh. "Why would you think somethin's wrong with me?"

He seems to study me a little. Then he looks around the room. "Dude, I don't know what the hell you're smokin'." He falls into the couch and then stops cold.

"Dude, what in the hell is that?"

I start to laugh. "Well, we've known each other since we were in diapers. I figured it was about time."

He looks at me with this stupid grin on his face. "Shit, buddy, then you should have gotten it in gold. Gold's more my style."

I just chuckle at that, as I watch him examine the ring.

"No, shit, though?" he says. "This is real?" It looks as if he wants to pick it up, but he's scared to or somethin'.

"It's real," I confirm. "I've already asked her dad."

"Shit! Have you asked her yet?"

"No, dipshit, that's why it's still here."

He looks at me as if he's still a little in shock, and then he picks up the black box and brings it to his eye level. "What? How long have you been thinkin' about this?" he asks.

"Since the first day I saw her."

"Wow," he exclaims. "This is real grown-up shit."

"Yeah, I know." I laugh out loud, and he just keeps lookin' at the ring. "So what do you think?"

He inhales and then exhales, and then his mouth slowly starts to turn up at its ends. "I think she'd be crazy to say no."

"Good," I say, nodding. I can feel the big grin frozen to my face. "Now, all I have to do is tell Owen."

Chapter Twenty-Six

Past

Rem

I get half the distance from the cemetery entrance to Owen's spot, and I stop.

"What are you doin' here?" I don't ask it accusingly or angrily. I just ask it.

The girl in the yellow sundress with long blond hair looks up at me, startled. The expression on her face looks just as confused as I feel.

I watch her tuck a piece of her hair behind her ear and then glance at the stone and then back at me. "I...I got back early, and I was just visiting an old friend."

Her gaze drops to the ground, and I just stare at her for a few seconds before commanding my feet to move. Then I walk a little closer to her and notice a postcard in her hand. And it hits me. Only then, it hits me.

"Ashley," I say, barely over a whisper. "How do you know Owen?"

There are tears in her eyes when she looks up at me, but now that I'm closer to her, I can see that they're not new tears. She's definitely been cryin'.

"I'm sorry," she says, wipin' her eyes with the back of her hand. "I didn't mean for you to see me like this. I was in the area, and I just stopped by. He was just a college friend." She laughs behind her tears. "Don't look at me. I probably look like a mess right now."

I don't say anything. I'm still just processing, my mind flashin' back to every single postcard I ever found lyin' against his grave.

"Why are you here?" she asks, after a few minutes of my silence.

I'm lookin' at the postcard. I'm tryin' to tell myself they were just friends or that maybe, in some twisted reality, she has the wrong grave. But with the postcard in her hand, I know she's got it right.

I take a breath and feel it roll back over my lips in shortened beats. "I'm here to see him." I gesture with my eyes toward Owen's grave.

A gasp falls from her pink lips. "You knew him?"

I don't say anything, mostly because I can't get my mouth to move.

"Of course you did," she goes on. "Everyone in this town probably knew him. I'm sorry." She pauses and then reaches for my hand, but I quickly move it away from hers. The action surprises even me. It surprises me how I could ever not take her hand.

"Rem? What is it?"

She's hurt. There's pain in her words. But I can't say anything. I feel my lips startin' to quiver, like they did the day I heard the news about Owen.

"Rem, it's not... I'm not... He was just a friend. I didn't mean to upset you."

She grows quiet again, but I can't stop thinkin' about her and Owen. I can't stop thinkin' about them together, about the postcards. She loved him. I know she did. She was the one who loved him. Ashley—my girlfriend, the love of my life—was the love of his life, too.

"Rem?"

I still don't answer her. I still don't look at her.

"Baby, how did you know him?" she asks.

I notice her flip the postcard around so that the photo is hidden by her dress.

"I'm guessing you were close," she says.

For the first time in...I don't know how long, I look into her tear-soaked eyes, and it's as if I don't even recognize her anymore.

"Baby?"

I hear the word fall from her lips, and this time, it stings every part of my soul.

"Baby?" She sounds as if she's startin' to cry again. Her word is broken and cracked—just like how I imagine we are now. It's as if someone just blew us both into glass, then took us and hurled us to the hard, dry ground.

Shattered.

We're shattered.

She starts to sob. I have to say something. I have to tell her.

I take a deep breath. Then I close my eyes, and I force out the words.

"He was my brother."

Chapter Twenty-Seven

Past

Rem

"*W*hat?" *Her word is breathy and bruised. "No,"
she says, shakin' her head, before I can even formulate
another thought.*

I'm stiff. I can't move. I can't even look at her.

*"No," she whispers. I can hear the tears in her voice.
"No," she says again, almost as if she can't quite believe it
herself.*

*I still don't move. I feel my chest pounding. It's almost
painful. I look at the gravestone that has my brother's name
etched into it. I look at the postcard she has pressed against
her dress.*

*My brother loved Ashley Westcott. Ashley Westcott
loved my brother. The words and their implications are*

sinking in. But maybe if I push them out before they have a chance to take hold, then maybe they'll just fade into oblivion.

I try to think of somethin' else. Ashley; the first day I saw her in the grocery store; her long, blond hair in waves; the way she looked at me; her smile, the same smile she probably gave Owen... I can't do this.

I turn toward the entrance to the cemetery, and I just start walkin'. She doesn't call after me. Of course, I don't know if I would have heard her if she had. I feel as if I have tunnel vision, tunnel hearing, tunnel everything. The black, iron fence that surrounds this place is closin' in on me. The sky, the dirt, the graves are all suffocating me. I've just got to get out of here.

I can't get to my truck fast enough. I reach for the handle, but I don't open the door. Instead, I lean my back up against its metal side and slide down until I'm restin' on my ankles. I feel the ring box in my pocket press into my thigh, and it sends an ache like I've never felt before sprintin' through my body. And just like that, I feel numb; I feel helpless. I came here to tell my brother that I was askin' the love of my life to marry me today. Now, it just feels as if I'm tryin' to hold water in my hand; that dream is slowly slippin' through my fingers.

I cradle my face in my hands. I've lost all control of my body. It's as if I'm losin' Owen all over again because I'm losin' Ashley Westcott—the only other person on this earth who might have known him better than I did. It all makes sense now. The more I gained of her, the more I gained of him. And if it all would have stayed a secret, she might have filled the piece of my heart that he took with him. But now that I know... Now that I know... I can't. I can't be with her. "I can't. I can't. I can't."

"Rem."

I hear her voice, and I drop my hands from my face. She's standin' in front of me, shakin' her head. Tears are chasin' each other down her cheeks and hittin' her chest.

"*I can't, Ashley.*" *I rise to my feet and face my truck. I can't even look at her.*

"*I didn't...,*" *she starts and then fades off.* "*I didn't know. Why didn't I know? Rem, why didn't I know?*" *she pleads.*

I try my damnedest to fight back the tears as my hand goes to the back of my neck. "*Everybody knows, Ashley. You don't have to look too hard.*"

"*Is that why you never said anything? Is that why no one ever talks about him around here? Everything! They talk about everything here. But nobody ever said a word about him.*"

I feel my gaze slowly liftin' in her direction. "*Believe it or not,*" *I manage to get out,* "*there are some things that are off-limits in this town. ...And he is one of them.*"

Then, despite my best efforts, my eyes wander over to hers, and my heart nearly breaks in half. "*I'm sorry, Ashley.*"

I reach for the door handle, and I pull the door open.

"*What?*" *She shakes her head.* "*Where are you going?*"

I drag in a long breath. "*Ashley,*" *I say in the calmest, steadiest voice I can muster,* "*I will fight for you.*" *I stop and correct myself.* "*I would have fought for you to the ends of this earth.*"

I can't bear to look at her sad eyes anymore, so I look at the ground at my feet instead before I continue. "*But I will not compete for you. I will not compete for you against my brother, my dead brother.*"

There's a stillness that comes between us then—like the calm before the storm.

"*Compete? Rem!*"

She cries the words, but I get into my truck anyway. And I sit there for a second and stare into the steering wheel. Is this really happening?

"Rem!" She's crying hard now; the ache in her voice is takin' over. A tear squeezes past my own eye. I can't leave her like this. Damn it, I can't leave her like this. But she was Owen's. She is Owen's. And she's still in love with him. I can't ever see her again.

I start up the truck.

"Rem!" I look up, and she's at my open window. "I'm so confused."

Her eyes are beautiful, even filled with tears. I want to hold her. I want to love her. I want to kiss her sadness away. But instead, I swallow it all down. And without another thought, I back out and peel away, leavin' a cloud of white dust and the love of my brother's life in my rearview mirror.

Chapter Twenty-Eight

Past

Rem

"*R*em.*"*

She climbs the three steps it takes to get up my porch stairs and pulls up a lawn chair across from me.

After the cemetery, I came here, and I haven't moved. I've just been sittin' here in this same chair for hours, starin' off into that blue horizon and thinkin'—back, forward, every which way.

"Rem, you need to talk to me. You need to tell me what's going on." Her eyes are red. It looks as if she's been cryin' all afternoon.

I don't say anything.

"Rem," she says, more sternly this time.

"What do you want to know?" My words cut at the air. They're angry. I'm sad that they're angry, but I can't seem

*to feel any other way. I just don't understand why I didn't
know. And I don't understand how she could have come here
knowin' what she knew and not say anything.*

*She takes a breath and then slowly exhales, just as her
eyes catch somewhere near my chest. "That was his jacket,
wasn't it?"*

*I look down at the old leather jacket, close my eyes
briefly and then slowly nod. "Yeah."*

*She presses her lips together like she's tryin' to hold
her emotions in. "Your last names?" she asks.*

*I swallow. I really don't want to talk about this. "His
dad and my mom were high school sweethearts. They got
married and had Owen. But not too long after Owen was
born, his dad passed away. Then a couple years down the
road, my mom married my dad, and they had me. My dad
raised Owen like he was his own, but Owen's really my half
brother."*

*I see her jaw drop right before she presses her hand to
her lips. "How? How did his dad die? He never told me."*

"Heart attack," I say, short and to the point.

*I glance at her, only to see the tears startin' again in
her eyes. Then I look away and focus on the bird feeder in
the yard. There's a lump in my throat, makin' it ache. I keep
swallowin', hopin' it will go away. I've never cried in front
of anyone. And I'm not doin' it today.*

Silent moments pass. She's quiet. I'm quiet.

*"Why did you come here, Ashley?" I still don't look at
her, even as I say the words. But as the moments draw on
where she doesn't say anything, I find my eyes wanderin'
back to her.*

*She's lookin' at me with a sad, puzzled look. "Rem, we
need to talk about this. We need to figure this out. I'm so
confused. I don't know how to feel."*

*"No," I say, "why did you come to Ava? You knew he
was from here."*

I watch her now. She bites her bottom lip and looks

*away to some spot off in the distance. "He talked about it,"
she says. It almost sounds as if it's a confession. "It always
seemed so magical, so peaceful. And I don't know, maybe I
just wanted to know the man I never really got to know. We
only dated for a few months. He was so quiet, so mysterious,
so..."*

*"I know. He was my brother." I say the words a little
too coldly. I hear them fall out of my mouth, and I
immediately regret them. But hearing her talk about my
brother... She knew him. She loved him.*

"Rem, do you think this is easy for me?"

*I don't say anything, and I still don't look at her. And
before long, I feel her hand touch mine, and as if it's almost
by reflex, I pull my hand back and lift my gaze.*

*Tears—one right after the other—are barrelin' down
her cheeks now. Her eyes are red. She's shakin' her head.
"Don't," she pleads. "Don't pull away like he used to. Don't
shut me out."*

*"No." I stand up and walk toward the steps that lead to
the backyard. "You can't compare us. He might have loved
you, but..." I stop and bring my hand to the back of my neck.
"I never did."*

*And if you can literally see a heart breakin' by the
expression on someone's face, I think I just saw Ashley
Westcott's heart break in half.*

"What?" Her word is soft and torn.

"I never loved you," I say.

And then, I turn.

And that's it.

My world crumbles, as I walk away.

Chapter Twenty-Nine

Past

Rem

I drift into Hall's and find a seat in one of the old stools at the bar. She's at my house. I didn't know where else to go. I just took off walkin', and two miles later, I ended up here.

"Rem." Kristen turns and looks at me. I avert my eyes. "What's wrong?" she asks.

"Bad day," I say, takin' off my cap and settin' it on the bar top. I don't even try to elaborate. How do you tell someone you've just lost everything?

Kristen pulls a beer from the cooler, opens it and then sets it in front of me. "You wanna tell me about it?"

I shake my head and take a swig from the bottle. "Not really."

"Okay," she says, noddin'. "You want me to call Jack,

so you can tell him about it?"

I look up at her. She's got this wry smile on her face, yet her expression is still somehow sympathetic. "No," I say.

Her lips quickly turn into a frown, and I realize I probably said that a little too harshly. "But thanks," I add, flatly.

"Anytime," she says, barely over a whisper.

I bow my head and stare at the worn, wooden bar top, thinkin' about what the hell just happened today. I still don't think I quite believe it all. Of all the people in this whole, damn world, it had to be her; it had to be my Ashley. Damn it, Owen.

I look up, and Kristen's still just starin' at me.

"Are you sure you're okay?"

"I never said I was okay."

Her shoulders rise and then fall in a breath.

"Is it Ashley?"

I don't say anything, though I'm pretty sure her answer's written all over my face.

"Real love bleeds, you know?"

I take another swig of my beer, set it back down and then habitually nod.

"That's how you know it's real," she says.

I try not to react to her statement, even though it hits my heart in an awkward place.

"Well, at least, fix your hair," she says, regaining my attention.

When I lift my eyes, she's givin' me a playful look. "You've got this Alfalfa thing goin' on."

I mindlessly run my hand through my hair just to humor her.

"Hold on," she says, leanin' into me. She takes both of her hands and runs them evenly through my hair. "There," she says, standin' back.

I chuckle. I don't even know where the sound comes from. It doesn't feel right. In fact, the motion of actually smilin' just makes my heart break even more because I realize then that I can't feel the smile. My mouth moves up, but my heart keeps sinkin'.

Just then, I hear the screen door slam, and Kristen and I both turn to see Ashley standin' in the doorway.

I immediately stand up. Ashley looks at me, and in one look, it's as if I can tell somethin' snaps inside of her. It's more than hurt. It looks like rage. She glances at Kristen but saves the longer look for me. And then she turns toward that screen door again.

"Ashley, wait!" I call out, but it doesn't do any good. I watch her blond hair fall in choppy waves down her back as she slides out the door. And then I freeze. What was that look?

"Rem."

Kristen snaps me out of my thought. I look over at her. There is guilt in her eyes now.

"I didn't... I mean, I didn't mean...," she stutters.

"Oh, shit," I say out loud, finally connectin' the dots. Did she really think somethin' was happenin' between me and Kristen?

I run to the door. I don't even remember goin' through it or runnin' halfway across the parkin' lot.

"Ashley!" I yell.

She turns, and the daggers in her eyes pierce right through me, forcin' me to fall back on my heels.

"How did you get here?" she asks.

"I walked." I'm still angry, but more so, I'm sad...for us. "You didn't know I was here?"

She crosses her arms over her chest. "I came here to talk to Kristen. I didn't come here to talk to you."

I take a sharp breath. Her words are ice cold.

"Ashley, it's not what it looked like...in there."

She shifts her weight onto her other leg, but her cold eyes never leave mine.

"Ash...," I stutter, before I stop. I want to tell her my

mind is such a train wreck right now that I don't know whether to cry or punch a wall...or laugh. But the words don't come.

"You were laughing," she says. "I don't think my eyes made that up. You tell me that you don't love me, and then, barely an hour later, you're here, laughing, like this was all just a game to you."

"Ashley, you know that's not true."

"I don't know what's true anymore." Her words slice at the thick air, and then just like that, silence fills the space between us. But she keeps her eyes in mine. They're piercin' right through me, causin' my heart to pound and my head to spin. I want to say somethin', but I don't know what to say. Every time I try to form a thought, an image of her and Owen fills my mind.

Long, tense moments pass like this before she shakes her head and drops her gaze from mine. And now, she just looks sad and almost scared. I want to take a step toward her, but I'm afraid, too. This can't work. It was doomed from the start.

One second.

Two seconds.

Three seconds.

Four seconds.

She looks up at me with a pair of soft, beautiful eyes, and it makes me want to go to her that much more. I love this girl, damn it! I love her. And I hate that I do—because she's not mine.

More seconds draw on. I don't know if she can tell what I'm thinkin', and I have no idea what's goin' through her mind right now. All I know is that there's this ache in my throat—as if I just took every soft kiss, every gentle touch, every sweet memory we ever made together and tore 'em to pieces and then swallowed 'em. Damn it! This isn't fair! I want so much to go to her. But I don't.

I don't go to her, and there's a look in her eyes that

tells me she knows that.

And that one moment—that one moment of idleness, when I chose to keep my feet planted... That was the one that sealed our fate.

She knows it.

I know it.

The color fades from her cheeks, and she gives me this look. I can't be sure of what it means; I can only imagine. I can only imagine it means: The end.

My heart breaks in half.

Our time's run out.

Chapter Thirty

Past

Rem

"Dude, did somethin' happen with you and Ashley last night?" Jack asks. He throws a log onto the pile and dusts his hands against his jeans.

I don't say anything at first. I just shove a few pieces of wood under my arm and walk over to the stack. But when he turns around and looks at me, I can tell he's waitin' for some kind of an answer.

I throw down the wood and head back to the dead tree we're cuttin' to pieces. "Why do you ask?" I say, tryin' not to sound as broken as I feel.

He hesitates. No one else might have noticed it, but I've known Jack all my life. That kind of pause means there's somethin' he knows that he doesn't want to tell me. I pick up *the axe from the ground and position a log vertically on the stump. And with one hard swing of the axe, the piece of wood falls into two.*

"She left this morning."

Without even thinkin', my gaze cuts to him. "What do you mean she left?"

He just stares at me. It's that kind of stare a man gets when he knows he's the bearer of bad news.

"She must have just packed up her car and left," he says. "I saw Karen in the bank this morning. She said Ashley was in there earlier closin' her account. I didn't really believe her, but when I drove by Ashley's place, it looked empty. Even that wind thing she had hangin' on the porch was gone—and so was her welcome mat."

I keep my eyes on him, as the words slowly, but surely, sink in. Then I lower my head, pick up another piece of wood, set it down onto the stump and swing the axe.

"Buddy," I hear him say over my shoulder, "I know I'm not the best at givin' advice...or at knowin' what to say or anything like that, but I've got an ear."

I set another log on top of the stump and swing—hard.

"We broke up," I say. I try like hell to make the statement sound as matter of fact as I can.

"You broke up?"

"Yeah." I don't bother lookin' up. Instead, I shove two big pieces of wood under my arm and walk them to the stack.

"What happened?"

I toss the logs down, one on top of the other and shrug. "It just didn't work out."

"But, dude, she left."

I ignore him, but I guess he takes that as an invitation to keep talkin'.

"Hey, I ain't no rocket scientist, but that seems like a little bit more than 'it just didn't work out.'" He holds up his fingers like they're quotation marks.

"Yeah, well, I don't know." I keep my eyes on the wood

pile, allowin' myself to think for a second. Damn it. Where the hell did she go?

"But you were gonna propo..."

"Yeah, well, I'm not anymore," I say, cuttin' him off.

There's a lump growin' in my throat. I try to swallow it down, but it doesn't go anywhere. And all of a sudden, I feel rods of pain start shootin' through my chest. I close my eyes and instantly feel dizzy. This is all becoming too damn familiar.

"You okay, buddy?"

It takes me a second to answer. "Yeah, I'm just gonna go inside for a minute." With that, I slowly stalk off toward the house, all the while, tryin' to take as deep of breaths as I can. But every breath feels as if it has to travel through a straw to get to my lungs. And by the time I reach the back door, my head is swimmin' in a sea of muck. She left? *I think it's all just hittin' me now. I can't be with her, and I know it. And I already know somethin' else, too: This is gonna be the hardest thing I've ever had to go through—and that's if I even make it through it.*

Inside, I fall into a chair at the table, simply because it looks closer than the floor. I was worried my legs were gonna give out.

I rest my elbows on the table and cradle my face in my hands. I feel lost. I never knew you could feel lost in your own home.

A handful of moments pass before I lift my head and let it fall back. At the same time, I exhale and will my heart to slow down for a damn second. Gone. *That word keeps playin' over and over again in my mind.* She's gone.

I level my eyes again and catch a light blinkin' on my phone.

Ashley.

In the next second, I'm reachin' across the table toward the light. It's a message. It's from her. My hands are shakin' as I click to listen to it.

"Rem."

Her first word comes soft and gentle, but it also sounds as if it's spoken through tears. The stingin' pain in my chest returns, and I press my other hand to my heart to try to curve it.

"I don't know," the message goes on. "I don't know how to feel." She stops there and tries to laugh, I think, but the result only sounds as if she's tryin' to hold back more tears. "But since you've made it so easy for me to leave...I'll make it easy for you to forget. I'm leaving Ava, Rem. I'll be gone today."

The message ends there. My hand holdin' the phone falls to the table. And I just sit there and stare; I stare at that phone's bright screen until it turns black.

Several months ago, I met a pretty blonde with a big smile, and I knew I had to know her name. Then once I knew her name, I knew it'd only be a matter of time before I loved her. And then once I knew I loved her, I knew I had to find a way to make her mine.

But then, that was before...

Now, all I know is that I have to find a way to forget her.

Chapter Thirty-One

Past

Rem

I pull up to her house. I had to see it for myself. I park my truck on the curb and step out onto the sidewalk. There's a letter in my hand. But I guess she'll never see it because that wind chime is gone and so is her love plant. It always used to sit on that desk right inside her front window.

I stop on the little concrete steps for a moment, replaying yesterday, remindin' myself why she's gone before I slowly make my way to the porch swing and sit down. Then I notice somethin'. That heart rock she found mushroom huntin' is restin' on the arm of the swing, almost as if she meant to leave it here—almost as if she knew I'd come back here sometime. I pick it up, turn it over in my hand and squeeze it against my palm. Then I put it in my pocket and focus on the letter.

I wrote it last night. I knew she was already gone, but there was a part of me that wished it were all just a nightmare or that she'd be back this morning.

I sit back against the wooden swing and unfold the page. Briefly, my eyelids fall over my eyes. I can feel the soft, late-summer breeze pushin' over my face. The air is thick with the smell of freshly cut grass and dogwoods. I breathe it all in. The air fills my lungs, but the smell is dulled. There's this fog that set in yesterday, and it makes everything feel less like it should. It clouds the scent of the grass and makes the leaves on the dogwoods look dry and dreary.

I unfold the letter in front of me. Everything I know is on this page. My eyes go to readin' over it one last time. And I don't know if I read it to force myself to feel somethin'—anything—or if I do it in hopes she can feel me sayin' these words somehow. I don't know why I do it, but I do it all the same.

My Confessions

Ashley Westcott, you are the most wonderful and special human being I have ever met in my life. Any guy would give anything and everything just to know who you are. I don't fault my brother for this.

Ever since the moment I first saw you, I knew that there was something incredible about you. You made me feel something that I had never felt before. It took me forever to gather enough courage to ask you out. You were...are...so beautiful. And I think there was a part of me that thought there was no way that you would be interested in me. But I had to try. I had to know you.

And then you agreed to give me a chance. And soon after, I got this feeling inside of me that was stronger than anything I had ever felt in my entire life. And the only explanation I had for the way I felt was that I must be in love.

Ashley, you have no idea what you mean to me. You are everything I could ask for and everything I never thought to ask for. You're smart and funny and sexy and gorgeous, inside and out. You're the whole package, babe. And I already miss you. I miss holding your hand—just feeling your touch warms my heart. I miss cuddling with you on the couch on those lazy Sundays and some Mondays, too. I wouldn't trade that for the world. And I miss the little things, like the taste of your skin, the sweet smell of your hair, the sound of your laugh.

And as I write this, I wonder if you're thinking about me. I don't think I'll ever stop thinking about you. The truth is, if you were here, I'd take you in my arms, and I'd hold you until you made me stop. I'm wishing... I'm wishing a lot of things right now. But mostly, I'm wishing I had met you first. And I know we can't change any of that. And to be honest, I don't know what that means for us. But I just wanted you to know that no matter what happens to us, you'll always be a part of me and you'll always have a place in my heart...always.

And...I'm sorry.

You deserve to know this.

~Rem

I finish readin', and then I carefully fold the letter. And then I fold it again. And I close my eyes until the only thing I feel is my heart beating. Then I rip the page in half, turn it, then rip it in half again...and again...and again, until it's just a bunch of little pieces in my hand. Then I squeeze the little bits of paper in my palm. And without another thought, I toss the pieces into the wind.

They hang in the air for a moment before gradually floatin' to the concrete and scatterin' every which way on the porch floor. I watch them for a few seconds dance in little circles in the breeze.

If everything were different, it would matter what I just did. But nothin's different, and that's not gonna change. My brother loved her first. And even if she doesn't still love him, I just can't do that to him. I just can't do that to my brother.

Chapter Thirty-Two

Present

Rem

I write the word. It's only one word, but it means everything to me, and maybe it will mean everything to her, too.

I set the pen down and slide the page of the book into the envelope. Then I seal it, turn it over and let it sit on the counter as I stare at her address—the post office box number I found in the back of the book.

It's not a novel; I didn't write a story about our life in my perspective. It's not a long letter explainin' myself or my reasons. It's not even a sentence. It's just one little word. It's just a simple answer—the answer to her question, the answer she needs to hear.

Chapter Thirty-Three

Present

Ashley

The return address on the envelope is his. Without hesitation, I quickly tear open its seal and slide the piece of paper out of the envelope.

It's the page of the book where I asked him the question. I see the torn edges on one side, and then I see my handwriting, and I stop there. My heart is racing. I close my eyes. Every bone in my body is aching to read what follows those two little words—*Was it?*—and yet, every fiber of my heart is begging me not to.

I slowly count to three in my head, but when I get to *three*, I keep my eyes closed. A million scenarios are running through my mind. What if he said *yes*? What if he said *no*? What if he didn't even answer?

I cautiously force my eyes open, and then I let them slowly crawl to the bottom of the page, until I see it.

It's one word—in his handwriting.

A breath tunnels through my lungs.

The page falls to the countertop.

My hand covers my mouth.

And instantly, I'm fighting back tears.

Chapter Thirty-Four

Past (1 Year Earlier)

*I stop at his spot and stare at his grave. I'm havin'
trouble formin' words. It took me a month to get back here. I
haven't seen him since I found Ashley standin' here with his
postcard. I just didn't know what to say to him.*

*But today felt as if it were just as good a day as any to
come out here. So, here I am. And after a while of just
starin' and thinkin'—about Ashley, about him, about my
childhood, about how my life goes on from here—I push out
a steady stream of air and then walk over to the milkin'
stool.*

*I take a seat and just sit there for a few more seconds. I
can feel liquid formin' behind my eyes. I clear my throat and
rub both my eyes at once with my first finger and thumb.*

"I'm sorry, buddy."

I try to swallow down the ache in my throat.

"I didn't know you and Ash..." I can't finish the sentence, so I take a second and try again.

"You know I never would have even looked at her that way if I had known."

I put my hand to my mouth and lower my head.

"I'm sorry, buddy." My eyes fixate on the ground, and then on his stone. "I'm sorry you're here. I'm sorry you can't be with her. I'm sorry I didn't talk you into playin' golf...or chess or somethin' a little safer than football. I'm sorry I ratted ya out to Mom that night you came home drunk. I didn't know any better, and I sure as hell didn't know anything about the brothers' code back then.

And I'm sorry we didn't name that dog Buster like you wanted to. It really was a better name than SpongeBob. I don't know how Mom and Dad let us do that to that poor collie.

And I'm...I'm sorry that I didn't show ya more that I loved ya." I pause and let go of a long sigh. "I'm sorry for that, buddy."

A drop of salty water escapes down my cheek. I quickly wipe it away and shift my weight on the little stool. And then I sit there in the quiet for a few minutes. The air is warm. The breeze feels nice. It pushes over the leaves in the tree next to us, makin' a calm, rustlin' sound.

"Owen, I've got a question for ya." I tug at the legs of my jeans and bend my knees. "And this wouldn't even be a question if this situation were different. And I'm sorry it's not different. You know I wish it were." I stop and take another breath. "But I guess it is what it is, and I just don't know what to do anymore. I'm at my wit's end here. I mean, I love her, Owen. I do. I can't stop thinkin' about her."

I pause and inhale a healthy dose of air. "But, um...I'll stay away from her...if you want me to," I say, in my next exhale. "I'll do it. It'll be hard, but I'll do it."

I take a second to wipe away the damn liquid that keeps

fallin' down my cheeks.

"But if, uh..." *I stop and bite at the inside of my lip before I go on.* "If there's still some way in this whole crazy mess we've made, where Ashley and I can still work... I mean, if that's even possible..." *I look down at my boots.* "Will you just, maybe, send me a sign or somethin'? I mean, it doesn't have to be a lightnin' bolt or any* Ghost Dad *shit or anything like that. In fact, please don't send lightnin' ...and please, please don't send a ghost." I laugh a little at that before I continue.*

"I don't know," *I say, glancin' down at his grave.* "That's probably crazy, right?" *I sigh and rub the back of my neck.* "Look at me, buddy. I'm goin' crazy." *I laugh again and shake my head back and forth as I do it.*

I've really got to get myself together.

I force out a breath and rest my hand on his stone.

"Buddy, I really wish you were here to help me through this. I could sure use some of your geezer wisdom right about now."

I smile, but then it quickly fades away.

"But honestly, Owen," *I say, restin' my forehead on the hand that covers his grave,* "what I could really use right about now...is a brother."

Chapter Thirty-Five

Present

Ashley

I park my rental in front of his house. It feels strange being back here—being here where he lives. There's a part of me that feels as if I shouldn't even be in this town.

I sit behind the wheel for a few minutes, just trying to talk myself into this. The radio volume is down, but I can still hear the low murmurs of people talking. Down the road, there's a girl riding a bike. It's a pink, Barbie bike with training wheels. I had one of those when I was little. The image of the girl on the bike makes me smile briefly. But soon, I'm taking in a long, deep breath and feeling the air slowly escape my lungs. I wish my heart weren't racing a million miles a minute, but it seems as though there's nothing I can really do to stop it.

I follow with my eyes the girl on the bike, until she disappears behind a bend in the road. Then, for some amount of time, I stare at the tree line that follows the graveled path. There's a soft breeze, causing the branches to sway in the wind. It's almost as if they're urging me to move.

"Okay," I finally whisper to myself. "You can do this."

I get out of the car and gently close the door behind me. The last thing I want to do is bring attention to myself.

I turn and look at the house. I look at its little white railings on its little white porch and at that same old swing that sways back and forth in the breeze now. That swing is almost identical to the one I had back here, which is no surprise. I swear everyone in this town owns the same porch swing.

I take a breath. I feel my heart pounding. I hear it beating against my eardrums.

You can do this.

I walk up the stone path, then I take the couple concrete stairs to his door.

I can do this.

I open the screen door, and then I hesitate momentarily before knocking twice on the storm door. It feels strange knocking, as opposed to just walking right in.

I step back then and let the screen door swing closed. There's a moment where I consider running. But my feet never budge from his welcome mat. Instead, I wait. I wait for several, agonizing seconds before the knob on the door starts to turn and the door slowly pulls open. And all too soon, he's standing there, staring at me.

And all I can do is stare back at him.

"Hi," he says, eventually.

I let go of a thankful breath. "Hi," I say.

He opens the screen door and takes a couple steps back. I'm guessing that means he wants me to come in.

"Um...," I start but then lose my words.

"I expected you," he says, rescuing me. "I mean, maybe not today, exactly, but eventually."

I smile, nervously. "I probably should have warned you," I say, stepping inside.

He shakes his head. "Nah. Storms need warnings. Ashleys don't need warnings."

My nervous smile turns a little less nervous.

"You wanna sit outside?" he asks. "It's a nice day."

I nod. "Sure."

I follow him out to the back porch, and he gestures for me to sit on the swing. I do.

He sits across from me on a lawn chair. It looks as if he hasn't shaved in a week. His hair is longer than usual, and his jeans are worn and torn. And his skin—his face, his arms, the parts of his legs that I can see through the holes in his jeans—is still dark and tanned from a long, hot summer. *He's beautiful.* But I try not to think about that.

"I guess I can assume you got my answer?" he asks.

I look up at him. "Yeah. You could assume that." My eyes fall to my hands in my lap. One hand is gripping the other so tightly that I can see my fingers turning red. "And I guess I can assume you read the book?"

He just nods and smiles. "You could assume that." His gaze stays for only a second in mine. Then he locks his eyes on something at his feet before returning his attention to me. "It was a good book. Though, I guess I might be a little biased," he adds.

176

"Yeah," I agree, trying not to smile, "you probably are."

A few quiet moments pass then, where I don't even hear so much as a bird sing. My eyes wander over to a dark circle in the floorboards. There's a million words running through my head, but I can't seem to put a single one into a sentence.

"Well, I guess you found your story then."

In an instant, my eyes find his. "Yeah," I say, starting to nod. "I guess I did." And that's all I say, but that's not all I want to say because that's not exactly the whole truth. The whole truth is that I wrote the book because I got tired of watching the sand of the hour glass drain out. I want to tell him that I wrote the book because I know now that the things we leave unsaid are the things that leave us the most broken. I want to tell him I wrote it because I was broken. I want to say to him that our fate might be set—that it might have been set all along, unbeknownst to us—but I needed closure. I want to tell him that I still need closure. I want to tell him all of this. But I don't.

"Rem," I say, instead. "I'm here because I wanted to say some things."

For a good few seconds he doesn't say a word. He doesn't even move—not even a blink. And I swear in that time my heart nearly stops beating. But then finally, he bobs his head. "Okay," he murmurs.

I let go of an uneasy breath. "I..." I start but then stop to gather my thoughts. "I wanted to say that I'm sorry I never said anything. I don't know why I kept it a secret. That was wrong of me." I find that dark spot in the floor again before falling back into his eyes. "I didn't expect to fall in love here." I pause and try to tame down the ache rising up in my chest. I think all the words I never said are finally hitting me—hard. "And I think once I did, once I did fall in love," I continue, "I was scared to tell you because I just knew you had to know him...some way. But I also think I was still praying that there was some tiny chance in this crazy universe that you didn't."

I try to read his expression, but I can't. And that scares me. I could always read what he was thinking.

"Ashley," he says, in a calm, rasping voice, "I'm...I'm not mad that you kept the secret. I mean, maybe I was at first, but..." He looks down at his feet and then back at me. "But I understand."

I watch him refit his cap over his head. "And I didn't mean what I said—that I never loved you," he goes on. "I just thought... I just thought it might make it easier for you to hate me."

"Hate you? Why would you want me to hate you?"

"I don't know. I had just found out you were in love with my brother. I just... I thought you were freaked out, too, and I guess I assumed you would want an out. I thought it would be easier for you that way. I just... I didn't know what to do."

"Rem," I say and then pause to suck in a quick breath. "I really liked your brother. And yeah, maybe on some level..." I feel my gaze wandering off to the tree line as my words trail off. "Maybe on some level, I loved him."

He shifts in his chair, and it forces my attention back to him. I know he's uncomfortable, but he's going to hear this—this time.

"For four months when I was twenty-one," I go on, "we spent a lot of time together." It looks as if he tenses up even more. And I don't know why I do, but I rest my hand on his knee, and thankfully, he lets me do it. "And yeah, he was hot-tempered and secretive and mysterious and quiet as can be. And I know you know that." He seems to relax a little. "He was nothing like you," I continue. "But I just keep thinking... I think I saw something in him." I breathe in deeply and then slowly force the breath out. "Rem." He looks into my eyes now as if he's clinging to my every word. "I saw *you*...in him. There was this piece of you he carried around with him. He never talked about his family. I'd ask, and he'd freeze up. I think he missed you guys. I think he secretly missed home—this place. Even though he never said it, I could tell he loved it here. And even though he never mentioned you specifically, I could tell he loved you."

I notice his Adam's apple bob up and down, and I squeeze his knee. "Rem, there was a piece of you in him. It was his good piece." I try not to tear up, but trying doesn't do me much good. "And I think I just kept trying to find more of you in him."

He swallows, and I think I notice his shoulders relax just a little more. Meanwhile, around us, the cicadas beat out a soft, slow rhythm.

"But I never loved him like I loved you," I say. "And to be honest, I think the feeling was mutual. I think we were just connected by a common thread all along. And I think that common thread was *you*." A small smile finds its way to my face. "It was you, Remington Jude. I was meant to find you. And I think Owen was meant to lead me to you."

He keeps his eyes in mine, but his lips are even, motionless.

"Rem, I might have loved him. But I was never *in love* with him."

He's quiet. I can tell he's thinking. His eyes are fixed now on something at his feet.

"Rem? What really went wrong with us?"

He looks up at me. "You mean, besides everything?"

I laugh softly but keep my eyes planted on him. "Did you mean it?" I ask. "The answer?"

He nods. "Of course I meant it." There's a hurt in his words; I can tell. I didn't mean it to hurt. I just needed to know.

"Ashley Westcott." He says my name and then drops his eyes from mine. I can tell his tongue is nervously playing with the inside of his cheek. But after a moment, his eyes return to mine. "I loved you more than I ever thought I could love anybody in this life..." He pauses for a second. "I loved you so much that when you left, I lost myself; I lost who I was." He starts to chuckle quietly to himself. "I didn't even know what bread I was supposed to buy anymore. And I didn't know what I did on Monday nights. I didn't know what I was supposed to do with an empty passenger's seat. Hell, I didn't even know what drink I was supposed to order at that fancy coffee shop in Parkville."

"You went there?"

"Yeah, once. But I got frustrated with all the words on the board I couldn't understand, so I left."

I press my hand to my lips and try not to laugh, even as my heart is breaking for him.

"But, Ashley," he goes on before I even have a chance to say a word, "bottom line, it's like I forgot how to be *me*...without *you*."

Tears instantly start spilling down my cheeks. I don't even know where they came from, and I don't try to stop them, either. "Why didn't you tell me this?"

It's as if he's trying to hold back tears now, too. "Because you already knew."

"No." I shake my head. "No, if I would have known..."

"You did know," he whispers. "I just hurt you too bad for it to matter."

Another renegade tear slips down my cheek, followed by another, and another. I quickly swipe them away with the back of my hand. But then he reaches across the space between us and runs his finger along my cheek, swiping away some of the saltiness. And there's a moment where he's looking into my eyes—a moment that I would swear I only imagined if I didn't know any better. But then it quickly vanishes like fog in the sunlight, and he sits back in his chair again.

"I'm sorry," I say, brushing away the last of my tears. "I just... It's nice to hear that." I drop my gaze for an instant, but then just as quickly, I'm swimming in the sea in his eyes again. "And I understand if this is too much for you, with him being your brother... I just... I came here to tell you that I'm sorry."

He doesn't say anything, but his eyes are so fixed in mine that it makes me nervous. I can't help but look down at the floor. There's too much in his eyes—too much I can't read, too much I don't understand. But after a moment, I feel my stare gradually gravitating back toward his. And it might sound crazy, but it's almost as if his eyes are spinning a web from his to mine now, so that I cannot look away. He must not know that I really don't want to look away—ever.

But then, something changes. And suddenly, the space around us fills with a dull, eerie hum. It's the cicadas. They're crying.

The sound fills my ears. I want to block it out, but I can't. And then, without warning, I see it. I see it scrolled across the whites in his eyes.

Our fate is sealed.

My heart sinks to the bottom of my chest, as I

anxiously search for words.

"I probably should get going," I say, my voice becoming shaky.

His gaze falters, and he nods.

Tension hangs in the air, and I hate it, but I don't know how to make it go away. I stand up and try to smile at him, but I don't think I'd even buy it.

"It was nice seeing you again, Rem."

He stands too, but still, just nods.

"Okay," I whisper to myself.

And then I turn to leave.

Chapter Thirty-Six

Present

Rem

"Oh," she says, stoppin' and turnin' back toward me. "I almost forgot." She reaches into her jeans pocket and pulls somethin' out. "Your key."

She sets the key onto the arm of the swing. "I know you really trusted me with this, even if you never locked your doors." It looks as if she tries to smile. "But that really meant a lot to me—that trust." Her eyes drop to the key before lookin' back up at me. "There are just some things in this world you don't take for granted. And that's one of them."

Instantly, somethin' makes my breathin' stop short. "What did you say?" I ask.

I watch little wrinkles form on her forehead.

"Your key," she says, eyein' the key again. "I'm sorry. I didn't even realize I still had it."

"No," I say, shakin' my head. "Not that."

I recognize just then that I probably sound crazier than a thunderstorm in January right about now. But all I can think about is that afternoon—that one afternoon, almost forever ago—when Owen said that same thing. I don't even know how I remember it. But he said: *There are some things in this world you just don't take for granted. And that is one of them.* And I know it sounds crazy, but all of a sudden, I get this peaceful feelin' inside of me. *Is this your sign, Owen?*

I snap out of my thought, and Ashley's starin' at me, like she doesn't know whether she should stay and help me or just run and save herself.

"Are you all right?" she asks.

"Yeah," I say, tryin' to shake it off as best as I can. "I'm fine." I let go of a wide smile, and I can tell she doesn't know what to think of that.

"Well, okay," she says. "I'm, um, gonna take off then...I guess."

She turns to leave for the second time.

"Ashley, wait." I reach out and grab her forearm, forcin' her to turn back toward me. This all might be a stretch, but I can't shake it.

I stare into her light green eyes. I don't know what I'm doin', but then, I know exactly what I'm doin,' too.

Moments tick away, and we're still in each other's eyes. There's a thick coat of uncertainty in the air, and there's no expression on her face whatsoever, so I have no idea what she's thinkin'. And I have no idea what she's feelin'. But it's her eyes. There's something in her eyes that gives me hope. And finally, I open my mouth.

"So, what are the reasons then?" I ask.

"Reasons?" she asks. Those little wrinkles return to her forehead.

"Yeah," I say. I take a step closer to her, and we both lower our heads. Now, I'm so close that I can smell the sweet, familiar hue of her perfume. It makes me think of her soft lips and the taste of her skin, and it takes me back to cool, lazy mornin's and long, hot summer days. I breathe it all in and try to hold it hostage in my lungs.

"What are the reasons we can't be together?" I ask.

And just like that, her eyes dart to mine.

"It's been a year," I go on, "and I haven't come up with a single one."

I notice her breathin' first. I hear it. I can almost feel her chest movin' up and down with each breath, but somehow, I can't tell if she's breathin' fast or normal or slow.

"Are you married?" I ask.

It takes her a second to answer.

"No," she softly says, still lookin' into my eyes.

"In a relationship?" I ask.

She slowly moves her head back and forth. "No," she whispers.

"Have you fallen out of love with me?"

She inhales sharply, and then her eyes leave mine for some spot off in the distance.

"Ashley," I say, regaining her attention, "have you fallen out of love with me?"

There's a moment that passes. Her chest inflates, and then she slowly breathes out. I'm scared to death of what she's about to say.

"No," she whispers. "No," she says again, briefly glancin' down before findin' my eyes. "I'm still in love with you, Rem."

In the next heartbeat, my arms are around her. I

gently press her head into my chest, and I just hold her. I hold her so tight. I want her to realize that this spot in my arms is hers—for the rest of our days here. And I can't help but notice that this doesn't feel strange or wrong, either. This just feels right. And soon, my lips are on her forehead, and I can feel the burnin' ache in my throat tellin' me that Owen gave me his sign. It all feels like a dream. I'm prayin' that it's not.

"I thought I had lost you." Her words are muffled in my chest. "I thought I had lost you, Remington."

I feel my voice channeling through my chest, long before I hear the words. "You never lost me, Miss Westcott. I was always here. I was always here...just waitin'." *Waitin' on a sign.*

I pull her even tighter into my arms and press my lips into her hair. "I'm yours, Ashley. I've always been yours."

Chapter Thirty-Seven

Five Months Later

"Tell me somethin' about my brother."

It's the middle of May. Ashley's head is restin' in my lap. The sun is dippin' low on the horizon, leavin' a stream of watercolors behind. And it seems as if the world is slowly fallin' asleep.

"You know the story about the cicadas and why they cry?" she asks.

"Yeah," I say.

"He told it to me once—when we were in college."

I smile and then let her words sink in for a minute.

"I know I told you I didn't remember who I had heard the story from," I confess. "But I did remember. I *do* remember."

She looks into my eyes.

"He told it to me, too—when I was seven," I go on. I push her hair back from her face. "My mom told him that it was his dad's favorite story. And I think because of that, it became his." I stop to smile a little. "And because it was his, it became mine."

We're both quiet for a moment, as I rest my fingers on the soft skin of her stomach—the part that isn't covered by her tee shirt.

"He said that the cicadas want what we have," she says, as if reciting his very words. "They want to feel fragile, breathless, alive. They want to feel the laughter in their chests, the pain in their hearts and the words on their tongues—even if those words will eventually fade away forever." Her gaze trails to the painted sky, and I follow it there as she goes on. "They want mortality because they see it as the greater dance. See, without *time*, the moments cease to be precious. And the moments matter—the blissful and the painful. Every. Last. One. They are what make it worth it."

I swallow down a laugh. "Damn, he was always more eloquent than me."

I can tell she tries not to laugh, too, as I go to strokin' her pretty, long hair. "Can I tell you somethin' you probably already know?" I ask.

"Shoot," she says, lookin' up at me.

"I wasn't always the best at tellin' you how I felt."

She lifts her brows, as if confirming my statement.

"But can I tell you somethin' you probably don't already know?" I ask.

"Okay," she whispers.

"I loved you with everything I had. Even when I said I didn't—even as I was saying the words—I loved you."

She draws in a deep breath and then slowly releases

it. I watch her chest rise and then gradually fall as she does it.

"Ashley Westcott, there wasn't a day my heart didn't go back to you." She smiles, and I just keep going. "There wasn't a day I didn't smell your perfume in the air and think of you or see a little, white Chevy and think I should chase it down. But I was just scared, I guess. I was scared I was betraying Owen. I was scared you still loved him. I was scared you'd never love me like you loved him."

I pause to collect my thoughts. "But as the days drew on, none of that really made any sense anymore. And in all of the fears that haunted me, I had forgotten one little fact: I loved you." I smile down at her. "I. Love. You."

"And maybe I'm too late to be your first," I go on. "But right now, I'm preparin' myself to be your last." With my fingertips, I trace a gentle line on her skin from her shoulder to her wrist. "I figure you should know that."

She keeps her eyes trained on mine as she finds my hand and presses it firmly to her heart. "I know that," she says, before she goes to nuzzlin' her cheek against my jeans. "I think there's a part of me that always knew that."

I laugh. "Then why'd we waste so much time?"

She looks up at me and smiles. "Because we're only mere mortals, my love."

I tuck another strand of her hair behind her ear. And then it's quiet, except for those cicadas cryin' in the trees around us.

"Rem?" Her voice is hushed.

"Yeah?"

"I think I know something else about your brother." Her words sound almost like they're a confession.

"What?" I ask.

"I think he was in love with Kristen Sawyer."

My eyes immediately cut to hers. "What? How do you know?"

She shrugs a little. "A girl just knows." Then I watch her pink lips turn up at their ends. "After I came here," she goes on, "I sort of put it all together. He had mentioned her once. And beyond the fact that he had mentioned her at all, he had also had this look in his eyes when he said her name."

I stare off into the distance, turnin' over her words. I mean, I guess we kind of guessed that, but I don't think I ever really believed it.

"It's just another reason," she says, "why I knew deep down that your brother and I would never really be anything more than just two people who shared a piece of this life for a little while."

I find her pretty eyes and gently rest my hand on her arm.

"I don't understand, I guess. I mean, he could have had her if he wanted her."

She shakes her head in my lap.

"No, he couldn't have."

"What do you mean?"

"Kristen's in love with Jack," she says. "Always has been," she adds.

"Huh," I say, in a sort of reflection. My head tilts back in deep thought. I knew Jack had a thing for her. I even suspected Kristen had a thing for him, but I guess I just didn't realize how deep it went.

I level my head again. "And Owen knew that?" I ask. She just nods.

"Wow," I say, still taking it all in. "Too bad Jack doesn't know it."

Immediately, her voice hitches in soft laughter. "I'm

sure they'll figure it out someday."

"Yeah," I agree, laughing too now. "I'm sure they will."

I slowly run my thumb down her arm. I just can't get over how soft and delicate her skin is, and I'm sure I probably never will.

"Rem?"

"Mm-hmm?"

"The mushroom hunting?" she asks. She looks serious now. "You didn't only go with your dad, did you?"

Instantly, I feel my chest inflate. "No," I confess, shaking my head.

"He was with you, wasn't he?"

I nod. "Yeah."

"It's your favorite memory because it's the three of you. Isn't it?"

"Yeah," I confirm.

"Why didn't you mention him?" she asks.

I look off at the sky in the distance and follow the blue as it fades to pink, and I think about her question. "I don't know," I whisper. "Maybe for the same reason he never mentioned me. I missed him. ...I miss him."

I look back at her, and I notice a look in her eyes that tells me she understands—that maybe she feels the same way, too.

Her gaze eventually wanders off to the horizon. I follow it back there, and I stare at that big, orange sun bein' swallowed up by the earth. Then, I remember somethin'.

"Why did you leave the postcards?" I ask.

She turns away from me and onto her side. I can't see her face anymore, but I hear her smile. "We talked about traveling around the world and seeing all the beautiful places. We said we'd do it someday. But until we got to *someday*, we would just stare up at that big sky, like two big kids, and we'd act like we were on a beach in Fiji or climbing some mountain in the Alps."

I let the words sink in before I open my mouth. "We are still talkin' about my brother, right?"

She laughs. "He was sentimental...at times."

I sit back in the bench and rest my hand in the curve of her waist. She's wearin' one of my old tee shirts. She's swimmin' in it, but she couldn't look any more beautiful.

And we fall quiet then, hypnotized by the cicadas' lethargic hum, pourin' through the trees and fillin' our ears.

"Rem, why do they cry?"

I eye the shadows underneath the canopy of the big oaks in front of us, and I smile.

"Because they want what we have," I say.

There's a pause, and then her voice comes out soundin' playful, yet somehow, I can tell there's a hint of soberness to it, too. "I'd still much rather be immortal."

I chuckle, and at the same time, squeeze her shoulder, right before she twists around and looks up at me. And I can almost see that Fiji ocean on that postcard in her eyes. "They want what we have," I say, tryin' to convince her of somethin' I know she already knows. "And that's why they cry," I whisper.

She takes her hand and starts tracin' little circles on my forearm with the tip of her finger. The way she does it is so sweet and comforting that it makes me want to hold onto this moment forever. But then, suddenly, her finger stops.

"Rem?"

Her eyes are starin' straight into mine.

"You're right," she softly says. "If I were them, I'd

be jealous of us, too."

I smile and pull her closer to me. She laughs and scrunches up her nose. "You know, baby," I say, "this love thing we've got goin' on here sure hasn't been easy." I kiss her sweet, soft lips. "And it sure ain't painless," I whisper into her ear.

She nestles her head deeper into my lap, then twists around again and looks off into the sunset. "But it's worth it," she says, into the wind. I can hear the smile in her voice. "But it's so worth it," she whispers.

Chapter Thirty-Eight

Rem

I hold a postcard in my hand. It's Saturday, June 22. Ashley is standing next to me. Her hand is in mine, and she's rubbin' my thumb with her own.

"Buddy, this is Ashley." I look at Ashley and then back at his grave. "I think you two have met."

I smile a little at that. Then I glance at the postcard again. The photo on the card is of the Grand Canyon. It's not Fiji...yet, but I know he would have liked to see it, all the same.

Ashley squeezes my hand. I turn the card over. There's handwriting on the back—Ashley's handwriting.

The Grand Canyon was beautiful. We know you would

have loved it. We miss you. Here's to hoping there's so much beauty in heaven that your eyes can't take it. With all our love.

Ashley's signature scrolls across the bottom of the card. Mine follows hers.

I wrap my arms around her waist and squeeze her against me before she takes the card and bends down to his grave. I watch her set the postcard against the stone, and then she returns to my arms.

"Sometimes I wonder," she says, barely over a whisper, "if I would take it all back—if I could, if that were even possible. Sometimes, I wonder if I knew then what I know now, would I sleep in the day I was supposed to meet him?"

She looks up at me. Her eyes are bright but thoughtful.

"But it makes me sad to think of not knowing him," she adds. "And then, it makes me wonder if I never would have met you."

Somethin' in the way she says her last words makes my heart swell. She squeezes my hand, and I nod because I agree with her. I want to tell her that I agree, but the words won't form on my tongue.

"I know, baby. I know," I manage to get out instead. And I do know. I know what she means. I'd take the pain every time, over not ever knowin' him at all. And I can't even imagine never knowin' this girl in my arms.

Several minutes pass, and then Ashley pulls away from me and gives me a light kiss on my cheek. "I'll let you guys have a moment."

I nod and squeeze her hand. Then, I watch her walk back to the iron gates, her blue sundress blowin' in the wind. And when she disappears into the parking lot, I turn back to Owen's grave. And I just stand there in silence, until a small smile fights its way to my face.

"Well, I did always wish you could have met her... And I guess I did always want to know who your mysterious girlfriend was."

I laugh a little under my breath as I shift my weight to my other leg.

"And I guess you already know she's somethin' special. I'm sorry I almost let her get away." There's a tear formin' behind my eye now. I try to wipe it away before it gets anywhere else. "But I promise you, I'll take good care of her, from here on out."

I take a step closer to him and place a hand on his stone. "I miss you, buddy. I know I don't always tell you that, but most days, I miss you like hell."

I take my hand back and stare at his name etched in that sandstone-colored rock before I take a deep breath and then slowly let it go. "Well, I better get goin'. We'll bring you another postcard of one of your places soon."

I start to turn but then stop. "And buddy..." My emotions are gettin' the best of me; I try to swallow them down, so I can get this out.

"Thanks for leading her to me."

A silent moment passes between us, and in the meantime, a renegade tear slides down my cheek. But this time, I don't bother to wipe it away.

"And don't worry, big brother, I'll make sure Jack takes care of *your* Kristen."

Chapter Thirty-Nine

Ashley

"**M**ay I have this dance, Miss Westcott?"

He holds out his hand.

I don't say anything. I just lay my hand in his.

"I could be mistaken," he says, taking my hand and resting his other on the small of my back, "but I believe it was three years ago today that I shared this same dance with you." I watch a wide smile slowly crawl across his beautiful face. "And this same song, too."

"You would not be mistaken," I say, giving him a small nod.

He draws me close to his body, and I gently rest my head on his chest, as we slowly sway back and forth to the music. I can feel his warmth. I can smell his crisp cologne; it reminds me that I'm home.

"And if I remember right," he goes on, "I believe we made our first rumor together here, too."

A smile forms without me telling it to. "I believe you're right about that as well."

Then I feel him press a soft kiss into my hair, and I lift my head from his chest.

"Would you like to confirm the rumors tonight, Miss Westcott?" He lowers his face to mine and whispers the words, his lips grazing my ear.

Before I even have a chance to process his question, he pulls away from me and takes both of my hands in his. And in one, fluid motion, he bends down and touches one knee to the hardwood floor.

I'm trying to wrap my head around this moment, but all I can see is his eyes. All I can see is him and the way he's looking at me. It makes me feel as if we're tethered together somehow, connected by some kind of imaginary line that runs between our hearts.

"First off, I think you left this with me a little while ago," he says.

He holds out a rock in the shape of a heart—the same rock I found when we went mushroom hunting together so long ago. I start to reach for it, but he pulls it back.

"It's yours, yes," he confirms. "But I'm hopin' you meant to give it to me." He shakes his head. "And I don't intend on ever givin' it back."

I just smile, while he stuffs the heart rock back into his pocket and pulls out a little black box. And I can feel my eyes grow wide as his next words come, honest and confident.

"Secondly, Miss Westcott, I fell in love with you here. I knew it. Miss Betty over there knew it." He eyes an older woman with gray hair in the corner, and I notice, for the first time, that the dancing has stopped and that every eye on or around this little hardwood floor is on us now. "Everybody saw it," he goes on. "I never recovered from that day. I've never loved another soul like I love you. I'm yours, Ashley Westcott, and everyone knows it. And if you'll have me, I'd love to continue makin' rumors with you for the rest of my life."

I just stare into his eyes. And my mind goes back. It flashes back to a warm summer night and a boy I'd never met. In the memory, my eye catches his. I don't look away. He asks me to dance. It's only a dance. And he's only a boy. But I'm lost. He holds out his hand. He doesn't know he's my rescue. I take it. And just like that, I rescue him back.

The memory fades, and when I come to, I'm nodding. I nod even before there's a question asked.

He laughs and still asks the question anyway.

"Will you marry me, Ashley Westcott?"

I can't stop smiling.

"Yes," I say. "Yes! Of course, yes."

He slides the ring onto my finger, and cheers erupt around us. Then he pulls me close and whispers in my ear the words I'll never forget for as long as I have breath: "I'm happy I have *the greater dance* with you, Miss Westcott. And yes...you're more than worth the scars those angels will someday see."

Epilogue

Ashley

One moment.

One moment can shape our entire life.

One moment; that's all it takes.

But the thing is, that's not the whole story.

The whole story is a little more complicated than that. For what really shapes our lives is more like a series of moments—one on top of the other. Like, it's not just *one* sunrise that shapes us, but all the nights before it. Just like it's not *one* cut to the heart that tears us apart, but all the memories that preceded it. It's a look on top of a thought, on top of a word, on top of a smile. It's a heart-pounding question, after a silent prayer. It's a slow dance, in the midst of a storm. It's a chance taken, even before

you're given it.
>It's a strange weave of tears and sweat and laughter.
>It's called life.
>It's about love.
>And sometimes, it's painful.
>But every time, it's worth it.

And the moments matter—the blissful and the painful.
Every. Last. One.
They are what make it *worth it.*

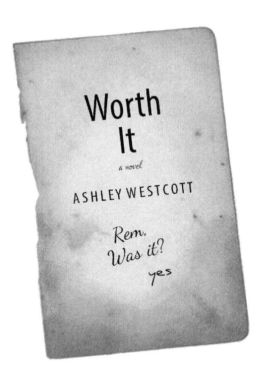

The End

ACKNOWLEDGMENTS

There are so many people to thank, and so many more beyond who are mentioned specifically on these pages.

First, I would like to thank God, my greatest inspiration, for giving me the opportunity to write for you.

And thank you to my amazing editors and sources for all your time and contributions. Thank you especially to Donna, Calvin, Kathy, April, Sharon, Jon and Jesse. Thank you from the bottom of my heart. Rem and Ashley's story wouldn't be what it is today without you.

I would also like to thank YOU, for reading. I know there are so many books out there. Thank you for taking a chance on my small-town characters. Thank you for taking the ride with them—for pulling for them, for cheering them on. And thank you for cheering me on! I, alone, cannot give these characters a life like you can give them. I might give them breath, but you give them a voice. You make them heard. Their story lives on through you. And for that, I am forever grateful. Thank you!

And a special thank you also goes to the amazing bloggers all over the world for their enthusiasm and loyal support and love of fairy tales. I know you don't have to do what you do everyday. I know, often times, your reviews are squeezed into a full day. But know that we, as writers, are so grateful for your commitment to literature.

I would also like to thank my family, including Jack, Aurora and Levi, who continues to be my biggest fans and greatest supporters. And thank you also to my friends and mentors, who are ever inspiring me.

And lastly but definitely not least, I would like to thank my husband, Neville. Thank you for your constant encouragement from the very beginning of this whole, grand adventure. Honey, I love you! And I'm so happy I have *the greater dance* with you.

Photo by Neville Miller

LAURA MILLER is the national best-selling author of the novels: *Butterfly Weeds, My Butterfly, For All You Have Left, By Way of Accident, When Cicadas Cry, A Bird on a Windowsill* and *The Life We Almost Had.* She grew up in Missouri, graduated from the University of Missouri-Columbia and worked as a newspaper reporter prior to writing fiction. Laura lives in the Midwest with her husband. Visit her and learn more about her books at LauraMillerBooks.com.

OTHER BOOKS BY LAURA MILLER
Butterfly Weeds
My Butterfly
For All You Have Left
By Way of Accident
A Bird on a Windowsill
The Life We Almost Had

"AN INCREDIBLE LOVE STORY."
~Justin's Book Blog on *Butterfly Weeds*

"THIS IS PURE ROMANCE AT ITS BEST."
~Kathy Reads Fiction on *My Butterfly*

"Newcomers will have their faith in good literature restored."
~Books to Breathe on *By Way of Accident*

"Completely and Utterly Beautiful."
~Back Porch Romance Book Reviews on *Butterfly Weeds*

"ONE OF MY FAVORITE LOVE STORIES EVER."
~A Novel Review on *For All You Have Left*

"Absolutely beautiful. Full of emotion. A MUST-READ!"
~Jenn and Books on *The Life We Almost Had*

"SWEET. LOVING. BEAUTIFUL."
~A Soccer Mom's Book Blog on *A Bird on a Windowsill*

91279300R00136

Made in the USA
Columbia, SC
19 March 2018